ONE MIDLIFE TO LIVE

Sweet Mountain Witches
Paranormal Women's Fiction Novel
Book Three

CINDY STARK

www.cindystark.com

LICENSE NOTES

DISCLAIMER:

All spells in this book are purely fictional and for fun.

Visit http://www.cindystark.com for more titles and release information. Sign up for Cindy's newsletter to ensure you're always hearing the latest happenings.

ONE

My doom was imminent. That was a fact.

I could barely breathe and could no longer run.

I'd let myself get out of shape, and this was the price I'd pay. If I survived, that would change.

Sweat trickled between my breasts, leaving me cold and hot at the same time. My heart thudded hard enough to make me wonder if it could explode from my chest, and I worried that I'd never be able to take a full breath again.

I should have gone straight home after work. Or stayed at my cat café. I should have known the danger I'd face by entering this woman's lair.

If I survived, I'd never make such a stupid mistake again.

Too exhausted to keep moving, I shot a quick glance at the blond-haired, lithe monster.

Victory flashed in her eyes.

She'd won, and we both knew it. I bent forward, trying to fill my lungs as I waited for fate to deal her hand.

"Alright, ladies," the fitness instructor said. "Let's take a quick break to hydrate and give those with less stamina a chance to catch their breath. Then we'll move onto squats."

Squats? What kind of purgatory was this?

I straightened and forced myself to walk on legs that had once seemed strong but had been reduced to jelly. I feared after squats, someone would have to carry me out.

To make matters worse, Mona Thompson, a sweet older witch from my coven with bright orange hair, seemed to be rocking the workout. Obviously, she wasn't moving at the pace of the younger women, but she also wasn't dying on the floor like me.

At the side of the brightly lit workout studio, I dropped to the tan-colored bamboo floor, leaned against the wall, and grabbed the water bottle from my tote. The scent of sweet lemongrass that filled the air along with the potted palms and fiddle leaf fig trees placed in corners had fooled me in the beginning, making me believe The Expanding Universe would be a lovely place to visit.

Oh, how wrong I'd been.

As I gulped down water, one of my best friends Nicole Santoro approached and sat next to me. Her breaths were labored, but nothing like mine, and a wide smile brightened her face. She tugged the tie from her dark brown curls, scooped her hair back again, and refastened it. "Oh, man. Karyn's tough."

I tried to huff my agreement, but only a little puff of air escaped. I inhaled and tried again. "Yeah. Brutal."

Nicole chuckled. "Still, she's fantastic. Stick with her, and she'll whip you into shape in no time."

I wrinkled my nose, showing my distaste for things that made me sweat and pant. "That's if she doesn't kill me first."

I jutted my chin toward the workout area. "How long have you been coming here, now?"

Nicole wiped tiny beads of sweat from her brow. "A couple of years, I guess. Ever since Karyn and her now ex-husband took over the old gym and upgraded everything."

"I should have started coming back then when you'd offered to be workout buddies."

Laughter danced in her dark eyes. "Better late than never. Speaking of, you were late to class. I'd started to wonder if you'd chickened out."

I didn't want to admit that I'd thought about it. "I stopped by my mom's. Been meaning to tell her about Gideon before someone else does. I tried, but I just...didn't. Couldn't? I don't know."

Even at my age, the thought of telling my mother that I lived with a demon was daunting. Not that I needed her approval, but I still wanted it.

She nodded solemnly. "You're worried what she'll say. About him being a demon."

I snorted. "I'm an adult. I can be with whoever I choose. But yeah, my life will be better if she and Gideon like each other."

A sudden smile appeared on her face. "Hey, now. That sounds like you've accepted that you'll have him as a permanent part of your life."

I shot her a look full of suspicion. "What do you mean by accepted?"

She grinned and bumped her shoulder against mine. "Anyone can see that you're meant to be together. Aeri and I are clueless as to why you've insisted on denying that."

The need to defend myself against the assumptions of my two best friends jumped to the forefront of my thoughts. "I didn't deny it. I just didn't know if he was the one for me. But maybe I do now. Assuming he wants the same."

She patted my arm. "You know he does."

Gideon hadn't spoken the actual words, asking me to spend my life with him, but I figured that he would at some point.

A petite woman dressed in bright kiwi green workout wear stole my attention as she entered from a side door and approached Karyn. While both women were about the same age and height with blond hair, the newcomer's dark roots were showing.

"Well, working out looks good on you," I said to Nicole as I watched the two women. Though I couldn't hear what they said, neither of them seemed relaxed.

She nudged my arm. "It'll look good on you, too, if you give it a chance. Every time you come here, it will get easier, and I'd love a workout buddy."

I struggled to produce a genuine smile and failed on a grand scale. "Yeah, that sounds *great*."

Truth was, if I wanted to fully embrace my new life, I needed to be stronger, physically. I couldn't predict when I might need to outrun another angry werewolf ghost.

The kiwi-clad woman swung her arm in a wide gesture, drawing my attention again. "Who's that with Karyn?"

Nicole searched the room for our teacher and smiled. "Oh, that's Liza, one of Karyn's friends. She teaches the yoga classes here."

"They don't seem to be too friendly right now."

Nicole studied them and nodded. "Yeah. I wonder what's up?"

Before we could plot any theories, Karyn turned her back on her friend and called us back to our places. Liza strode out the door. I drained the last of my water bottle, placed it in my bag, and dug deep for any remaining energy that I might have.

Karyn ruthlessly pushed us for the next twenty minutes, and by the time we'd finished the workout, I was certain I wouldn't be able to walk in the morning. I pulled the water bottle from my bag and realized I should have saved some for after the class.

I held the empty bottle up for Nicole to see. "I'm going to refill before I head to the showers. Meet you there."

I slid my bag onto my shoulder and headed in the opposite direction from everyone else, to the foyer where the water fountain also had a bottle-filling station. My heart rate slowed as I walked, and the blessed euphoria from working out kicked in.

At the fountain, I set my bottle beneath the spout and pushed the button to dispense water. When it was halfway full, I paused to quench my thirst before I continued filling it. Voices echoed from somewhere nearby, but I didn't see anyone as I headed toward the locker room until I reached the hallway leading the studio.

At the dark end of the hallway, I caught sight of a well-built man with dark hair wearing a black tank top that showcased his biceps. He and the yoga teacher had ceased talking, and he now had Liza pressed against the wall as they engaged in a passionate kiss.

I widened my eyes in surprise and darted into the studio, not wanting to find myself in the awkward position of interrupting them. From there, I headed straight for the shower, mopping the sweat from my forehead as I did.

When I finished washing, I turned off the water and wrapped a fluffy green towel around me. I emerged and found that Nicole was nowhere in sight. In fact, most of the women had already departed, leaving me alone in the locker room with Tamra Church, a timid, petite woman with wispy blond hair, who stood at a sink washing her hands.

She glanced up in surprise and caught my reflection in the mirror. She quickly looked away, grabbed her bag that had been sitting next to the sink, and hurried from the room. All without drying her hands.

I frowned. I wasn't an especially outgoing person, either, but it seemed rude not to respond to the people around me with at least a smile or a nod.

As I dressed, I planned out the rest of my evening. After that workout, I'd certainly earned a glass of wine. I could cuddle up on the couch with a good book. Or better yet, I'd sit with Freya and see if I could figure out how to strengthen our communication.

I had no idea if Gideon would be home since his work had been calling him away more often than usual. I wondered if it had anything to do with the demon on his team who'd gone rogue, but I hadn't found the courage to mention it. His job had become the "don't ask, don't tell" elephant in the room, and it seemed neither of us wanted to acknowledge that.

Still, if we were to ever move beyond roommates who'd had a few stolen kisses, we needed to be open and honest with each other, and I felt strongly that the issue had to be a priority in my life. I'd been doing everything to keep him a secret from everyone but my two best friends, and Gideon and I deserved better than that.

A horrified scream interrupted my thoughts, leaving a cold chill creeping up my spine. The unnerving cry seemed to have come from outside the locker room, and it sounded as if someone was hurt. Or terribly scared.

I immediately worried about Nicole and knew there was only one way to find out what had happened. I dug in my purse for my phone and the magic-infused pepper spray, just in case, and then slammed the locker shut.

As I made my way into the hall, the sounds of a woman sobbing drifted toward me, and I hurried in that direction. When I reached an office with the lights on, I cautiously peeked around the corner and found Liza holding a cellphone to her ear and an exercise band in the other hand. She still wore the kiwi green workout gear I'd seen her in earlier, and she stood next to a desk overloaded with clutter.

When she spotted me, she flinched and released another ear-piercing scream. The exercise band dropped to the floor with a thud.

Her scream startled me, and I held up a hand. "It's okay. It's just me."

Liza looked at me with wild eyes.

"What's wrong?" I asked, my voice now sounding as frantic as hers.

She shook her head at me and spoke into the phone sounding breathless. "No, it's...someone's here to help. I...I don't know if we're safe."

She kept her gaze locked on me as though if she blinked, I might leave. She listened to whoever spoke to her and then shook her head furiously. "I don't think I can stay in here with the...*body*."

Body?

I jerked my gaze toward the desk, the only place in the room where I didn't have a clear view. The tips of a pristine pair of white athletic shoes poked from behind the desk, and I inhaled sharply. "Oh, no."

Nicole had brand new shoes.

Icy dread gripped me with its claws. I swallowed and moved closer. I needed to see who it was but didn't want to look at the same time.

When I found that it was Karyn, not Nicole, who lay crumpled on the floor, a mixture of relief and horror twisted inside me. Karyn's body was sandwiched between a white leather office chair and the desk, as though she'd been sitting or about to sit when she'd died. Skin that was once pink with vitality now appeared lifeless and blue.

I pushed the chair back to make room, intending to check for a pulse. But then I noticed the bruise encircling her neck, and I feared she'd been strangled.

I thought of the exercise band that Liza had dropped. Then turned and looked at her in horror and disbelief. "Did you kill her?"

She widened her eyes as though shocked. "Oh, my God, no. *No.*"

Liza melted into a pool of sobs and tears, dropped her phone on the desk, and hurried into the hall. "I can't handle this," she cried.

I picked up her phone and followed her. She'd crumpled against the far wall with her knees bent to her chest and her head down.

I could hear a voice demanding attention from the phone and looked at the screen. She'd called the police department.

"Hello? This is Daisy Summers."

The dispatcher seemed to be relieved to hear my voice. She assured me that officers had been dispatched and would arrive momentarily. Then she asked me the same question that she must have asked Liza.

Were we safe?

Honestly, I had no idea if the murderer was still close by or if, in fact, I was looking at her. But I had my pepper spray, and, after my previously terrifying encounter with a werewolf's ghost, I'd studied up on protective spells.

I exhaled deeply. "I think we're okay."

Nicole turned the corner into the hallway, startling me and Liza all over again. At least the distraught yoga teacher didn't scream a third time.

I waved Nicole forward and then pointed at Liza, motioning for my friend to help her while I finished the call. "Other people in the building are starting to arrive, too," I said into the phone. "We should be okay until officers get here."

The dispatcher asked me to keep the line open until they arrived. I agreed and set Liza's phone on the floor near her.

The ringtone from my own phone followed closely afterward. I knew who it would be and why Gideon was calling, and I loved him for checking on me. I fished the phone from my pocket and answered.

"Are you okay?" he asked, his voice deep and thick with concern. I pictured him at home on our couch with my cats snuggled up to him. His dark hair would be slightly tousled in a sexy way, and his eyes the color of a clear blue lake were likely dark with worry.

I hated that Gideon had to check on me every time I experienced anything alarming, but since I'd become a possible target for a rogue demon, I did appreciate it. "Yes, I'm fine. Don't worry. Someone died at the fitness studio, but help is on the way."

Nicole widened her eyes in terrified surprise. *"What?"*

I lifted a finger to tell her to hold for a moment, and she looked at me as if I was insane.

Liza tried to speak, choked on her words, and began to cry in earnest again.

The situation was deteriorating fast. "I need to go, Gideon. I promise I'm fine, but others need my help. Police are on their way, and I'll call as soon as I can."

He acknowledged my need, ended the call, and I turned to my pale friend. I wished there was a way to lie to Nicole so that she wouldn't have to witness what I had, but there was no getting around this. "Karyn is behind the desk. Dead."

Nicole's hand flew to her mouth. "No. *No. What happened?*"

I glanced from her to Liza and back again, wondering the same thing. "I think someone killed her."

TWO

The dispatcher was correct, and the police arrived only minutes after Nicole briefly stepped into the office. When the sirens sounded like they were on top of us, I lifted Liza's phone to let the dispatcher know and disconnected the call.

Nicole and I held each other's gazes, our eyes mirroring disbelief. We both had questions, but it seemed like the wrong time to discuss anything while we stood over Liza as she grieved for her friend.

Or at least her prominent emotion appeared to be grief.

I'd begun to wonder if the bright green resistance band lying near Karyn's feet might have been the murder weapon. If so, it was more than a little suspicious to have found Liza holding it as she'd stood over the body when I'd walked in. The speed with which she'd quickly dropped it was also suspect.

The sounds of multiple voices reached us, and I was relieved to know that officers were on the scene. I stepped into the hall to let them know where we were, and Corey Shelton, Sweet Mountain Meadow's police sergeant and my childhood crush, turned a corner and met my gaze. Another much younger officer, a man with a medium build, light brown-hair, and Eaton on his uniform's name tag, accompanied him.

Corey's look of disbelief quickly turned to concern. "Daisy? What are you doing here?"

I opened my hands wide, astonished that I was at another crime scene as well. "I'd come with Nicole for a class, but I'm starting to wonder if I'm cursed. This is the second dead body I've come across in as many months."

He glanced at the young officer with him and lifted his chin. "Secure the scene."

The man gave a quick nod and took off.

Corey approached me and lightly gripped my upper arm as he studied my face. Then he focused solely on my eyes. "You okay?"

A shiver raced through me as the reality of my situation hit hard. "Yeah. I'm alright."

I gestured toward Liza sitting against the wall with Nicole kneeling next to her. "Liza's the one who found Karyn and called the police. Nicole and I came running when we heard Liza's scream. Karyn's...body is in that office."

He passed me and strode into the room. I followed, and once we were inside, I caught his arm, drawing his gaze. I leaned close to speak in a hushed tone, but I accidentally caught a whiff of his incredible cologne and was unable to keep from taking a deeper breath.

Corey adjusted the ball cap covering his blond hair and tilted his head toward me. I found myself unnervingly near to him, close enough to study the few strands of gray that hid amongst the blond hair next to his ear.

I steadied myself and whispered. "I think Karyn might have been strangled. When I first found Liza, she was holding that green resistance band that's on the floor. I don't know if it means anything, but I thought you should know."

He straightened, and his blue-eyed gaze met mine. "Thanks, Daisy. Let me get the scene secure, and then I'd like to talk to you in more detail."

I ignored the attraction pulsing between us and nodded, wanting to offer as much help as possible. "Of course."

Feeling awkward, I stepped out. I knew he liked me. And he knew that I was with Gideon, but that hadn't stopped him from making it clear that he'd be around if things didn't work out.

Two more officers rounded the corner including Sofia Doyle, a regular customer at my coffee shop. Officer Kemp, a muscled, bald veteran of the Sweet Mountain Meadows police department accompanied her. Officer Doyle stood as tall as me, but her blond hair sported strands of red, not silver like the ones hidden in mine.

She drew her brows when she spotted me, and I knew she mentally questioned why I was at yet another crime scene. Still, she only hesitated a moment before she followed her counterpart into the office.

I heard Corey instruct Kemp to help Eaton secure the building. Then he charged Sofia to locate a suitable spot to gather the witnesses. She emerged from the office, looked me over, and then glanced down at Nicole and Liza. "Follow me."

Officer Doyle led us back to the main fitness room where Nicole and I had sweated it out earlier. The room had been brightly lit then, but when we entered, half the lights had been turned off. It wasn't so dark that we needed more, but the dim atmosphere left me unsettled.

Sofia led us to a row of chairs that rested against the back wall. "Take a seat."

As we did, she gripped the backs of two empty ones and dragged them to the other side of the room. When she returned, she focused on Liza. "Let's start with you."

The blond-haired, petite woman sobbed in earnest as she stood and followed Sofia to the two chairs, leaving Nicole and me alone. I strained to hear what the officer said, but they were too far away to hear anything but murmuring.

Nicole stared at me with wide eyes. "What even just happened, Daisy? This is insane. I can't wrap my brain around the fact that someone might have killed Karyn while we were here."

I sagged against my chair. "I don't think might is the correct word, Nicole. I'm almost certain that Karyn was strangled with that exercise band."

She frowned. "Exercise band?"

"Yeah, the one near Karyn's body. Liza was holding it when I walked in and then dropped it. Didn't you see the trauma marks around Karyn's neck?"

Nicole lifted her brows and shook her head briskly. "No. I didn't notice. I only glanced at her."

Which was for the best. No need to have that image unnecessarily seared into her brain.

Voices in the hallway drew our attention, and I turned to see the young officer who'd arrived with Corey enter the room. Bobbi Knowles followed him.

I knew who she was, though I'd never spoken to her other than a hello on the street. Still, she'd always seemed friendly enough, and I seemed to recall that she worked for Karyn in some capacity.

At the very least, I knew their daughters were friends because I'd always see the two teenagers with long blond hair walking together along Main Street after school. They often dressed similarly, and I wouldn't have been surprised if someone had mistaken them for sisters.

Bobbi wore an old t-shirt and had pulled her brown to blond ombre hair into a low ponytail. She was thin, almost too thin, and fear dimmed her expression.

When the officer reached us, he pointed to the chair next to me. "Have a seat. Officer Doyle will speak with you shortly."

As Officer Eaton strode away, Bobbi sat and caught my gaze. "What's going on? Why are the police here?"

I drew my brows together. "Didn't you hear the screams?"

Bobbi shook her head frantically and lifted one of the earbuds that hung on the cord over her shoulders. "No, I was listening to music while I cleaned. Did something happen?"

I sent her a look full of compassion. "I'm so sorry to tell you. It's Karyn."

Bobbi looked from me to Nicole and back again, seeming confused. "What happened to her?"

I focused on her face, prepared to watch for any signs of guilt. "Karyn died, Bobbi."

She opened her eyes wide and gasped in horror.

Then she went limp and toppled from her chair to the floor, landing with a soft thud.

It took me a second to register what had happened.

Nicole echoed Bobbi's gasp, and we both jumped from our chairs and knelt next to Bobbi. Carefully, we rolled her onto her back. Her chest rose and fell in shallow breaths, and I thanked the Goddess that she was still breathing.

Nicole stood and called out. "Help! We need help. Bobbi's down."

Officer Doyle and Liza looked up with startled gazes and rushed from across the room. The cop had her finger on her shoulder mic as she did, her voice sounding urgent as she called for assistance.

Sofia reached us, dropped next to me, and lifted Bobbi's wrist to check for a pulse.

"She's breathing," I said before she could ask.

"What happened?" Sofia demanded.

"I'm sorry. She asked why you were all here. When I told her Karyn had died, I guess the information was too much for her, and she passed out."

Corey and Officer Eaton charged into the studio from different doors on opposite sides of the room. "What happened?" Corey demanded, sounding much like Sofia had seconds earlier.

Sofia nodded to me with a toss of her head. "She informed Bobbi of Karyn's death. The shock must have caused her to faint. She appears to be stable, and medical assistance is on the way."

I lifted my gaze to where Corey towered over us and mouthed that I was sorry.

He blinked and turned to the younger officer. "Did you secure the scene?"

Officer Eaton gave a quick nod. "It's all clear, sir."

Corey removed his jacket and placed it over Bobbi's torso. I tucked it in around her just as Officer Kemp strode into the room with his hand wrapped around the bicep of an equally built man. One who I was certain was the guy I'd seen kissing Liza.

Corey stood and turned to Officer Eaton with an incredulous look.

The younger officer blushed. "I meant *my side* of the building was clear. No one else is on the premises. On my side," he clarified again.

Corey shook his head, obviously disappointed. "Communication is key in this line of work, Eaton. It can mean the difference between life and death."

Officer Eaton nodded furiously. "Yes, sir."

Corey turned to Officer Kemp. "Is this the only other person on the premises?"

He nodded. "I believe so, but I'll make another sweep of the entire building."

Bobbi roused moments later, before the ambulance's arrival, looking dazed and confused. She glanced at all our faces and then focused on mine. "What happened?"

I sent her an apologetic look and took her hand. "I think you fainted from shock."

She struggled to inhale. "Oh, God, Karyn. I don't understand. I just saw her. Not long ago. She can't be—"

Her voice broke on a whimper of pain. She brought her hand to her mouth and squeezed her eyes shut, pushing a stream of tears down her cheeks.

Corey knelt next to me and placed a hand on Bobbi's shoulder. "You knew Karyn well, right? You worked for her."

Bobbi opened reddened eyes. "I clean for her. Here and her house." She paused to inhale an emotional breath. "But we were more than that. We were friends."

Two young women paramedics came through the doors then, one carrying a large bag while the other wheeled a stretcher. Corey wrapped his fingers around my arm and motioned that we needed to move. The medics tended to Bobbi, checking her vitals, and asking her questions.

Corey directed Sofia to continue questioning us and told Officer Eaton to accompany him, back to Karyn's body, I suspected.

Before they could act, though, Bobbi spoke out, her tone carrying above other voices. "*No.* I don't want to go."

The shorter of the two medics rubbed Bobbi's upper arm. "It's a good idea to have a thorough check-up, ma'am. Just to make sure your heart is okay and that you didn't hit your head when you fell."

Tears leaked from Bobbi's eyes. "I can't afford it."

I stepped forward. "I can drive her to the hospital so that she doesn't have to worry about an ambulance bill."

Bobbi shook her head. "No hospital, either."

The other blond medic crouched down. "You have the right to refuse, but we still highly recommend that you see your doctor today. It's in your best interest, ma'am."

I raised my hand. "I'll be happy to drive you, Bobbi. Please let me. You've had quite a shock."

It was the least I could do since I'd contributed to her current condition.

Corey nodded at Bobbi, letting her know she should accept.

Bobbi blinked several times. "Okay. I guess."

Corey agreed to let me accompany her as long as I promised to stop by the police station afterward to give my statement.

I assured him that I would. "Let me get my purse from the locker room."

As I walked out, I noticed the muscular guy wearing the black tank top watching Liza. She looked in his direction, and he quickly averted his gaze. Her expression turned to one of despair before she clasped her hands together and studied them.

Odd behavior, I thought, considering they'd been very friendly with each other not long before.

Then the man shifted his gaze to me and stared as I walked out of the room, leaving me with an uneasy feeling.

THREE

When Bobbi and I emerged from the fitness studio into the cooled evening air of Sweet Mountain Meadows, I spotted Gideon leaning against the side of the building. He and I were technically living together now and I saw him daily, but the sight of him always jolted my heart and made me ache to reach out and touch him.

Gideon immediately straightened and headed toward me. "Hello, my lovely."

His presence startled Bobbi, and I gave her a reassuring smile. "Bobbi, this is my...friend Gideon. Gideon, this is Bobbi. She's had a bit of a shock, and I'm taking her to the doctor to make sure she's okay."

Gideon tipped his head in greeting. "I'm very sorry to hear that, Bobbi."

She wiped tears from her eyes and gave him a careful smile. "Thank you."

I pointed toward my car. "Let me get her settled and then I can talk, but only for a second."

With Bobbi in the car, Corey's jacket still around her to keep her warm, and the door shut, I turned to Gideon. "I'm sorry you came all the way down here. I told you I was okay."

He gave me a gentle smile and drew his thumb down the side of my cheek, leaving me with shivers. "I know. But I needed to see for myself. I'd sensed that something bad had happened, and then you'd said someone died."

I dropped my shoulders in dismay. "Yeah. Karen Strickland, the owner and cardio instructor here, was found dead. I'm almost certain her death wasn't accidental. When I told Bobbi about her friend, she fainted, so I'm taking her for medical care."

He drew his brows together in a frown. "That's disturbing to hear. Do they have the killer in custody?"

I shrugged. "Not yet. Hopefully before the night is over. I really need to go. Can we talk when I get home?"

A slow smile curved his lips. "Yes. I'll see you when you get home."

Something about the way he said it made me think he took great pleasure in knowing that we inhabited the same house. I mirrored his expression and placed a hand on the side of his cheek. "Thank you for caring."

His gaze burned into mine. "Always."

From out of nowhere, the urge to kiss him overwhelmed me. I stood on my tiptoes and brushed my lips against his. "See you soon."

I headed for the driver's side of my car and glanced at him again. He placed two fingers on his lips and then pointed them toward me.

The air rushed out of my lungs and left my head swimming. I opened the car door and dropped onto the seat before the man devastated the last of my remaining senses.

Bobbi watched me with a curious gaze.

I wasn't sure what she was thinking, and I likely didn't want to know. "Let's get you to the doctor."

I called ahead to the medical clinic to be sure that they could see her immediately, and then I pulled out onto the street. The fitness studio was at the opposite end of town, but even with that, it wouldn't take long to get there.

Bobbi had stopped crying for the time being, but the emotional trauma we'd both experienced hung thick in the air. "Is there someone I can call, someone that you'd like to be at the clinic with you?"

She shook her head.

"What about your daughter?"

"Alisha doesn't need to be tangled up in this. I'll be fine."

Except Bobbi wasn't fine. Stubborn, though. I silently mouthed a calming spell and hoped that would help.

A few moments later, she exhaled a deep breath, which was a good sign. "I can't believe Karyn's truly gone. Are you sure? Did you see her?"

I nodded in the darkened interior. "Yes, I did."

Bobbi remained quiet for several moments before she spoke again. "Do you know what happened? How she died?"

I gave a small shrug. "All that I know for sure is that I heard Liza scream, and I found her in Karyn's office with Karyn lying on the floor."

Bobbi sniffed and turned to me. "Did you check to make sure she hadn't just passed out or something like I did?"

I cast a gentle smile in her direction. "I'm certain that she's passed on, Bobbi. I wish I could tell you otherwise."

She inhaled a ragged breath and whimpered. "I just can't believe it. This must be a nightmare."

I placed a hand on her forearm and squeezed. "Try not to think too much right now. Just focus on you. Everything else can wait."

Bobbi shook her head. "I just...she was too healthy for a heart attack. I don't know what else it could be."

I swallowed and prayed I wasn't making another mistake by telling her. "I think someone might have killed her."

Bobbi's intake of breath was strong and swift. "*No.* In her office? With all of us around?"

I turned into the parking lot of the medical center and parked beneath a light that illuminated the inside of my car. I shifted in my seat to face Bobbi. "I could be wrong, but I don't think so. Do you know of anyone who might want to harm Karyn? Did she have enemies?"

Bobbi clenched her jaw and glanced from side to side as though waging a war in her mind. "Not really. Not enough to take her life."

Her words didn't exactly convince me. "But..." I offered.

She met my gaze with a worried expression. "Liza?"

The one word sent my pulse racing. "Why do you suspect her?"

Bobbi shrugged. "I guess because they'd been arguing a lot lately."

I drew my brows in question. "Any idea why?"

She hesitated a moment and then shook her head. "No, not really. There was just a lot of contention there. Lately, Karyn was always in an awful mood after she'd been around her. Ask Liza. Maybe she can tell you."

I had a feeling Bobbi might have been holding back, but maybe she truly didn't feel she had enough to say anything specific. One thing was for sure, though. I was tempted to ask Liza that question myself.

I held Bobbi's elbow as we walked through the darkened evening. Enough light had faded to bring the shadows out to play, and I stared up at the mountain looming above us. Somewhere, part of the way up, Gideon was waiting for me, and I suddenly wished I was already home.

I'd been involved in two murders since I'd met him. The first one, I'd had to search for the murderer or risk being accused myself. The second, I'd been dragged into it and mostly had no choice. And while I enjoyed solving the mysteries, they had also brought a lot of drama into my usually quiet life.

Maybe I didn't want to ask Liza after all. Maybe I wanted to pass things along to the authorities and leave it all there. I had enough to occupy my attention with worries about Gideon, settling into my new home, and my new coven duties.

Inside the medical center, I assisted Bobbi getting checked in. The kind nurse in reception insisted that Bobbi sit in a wheelchair since she'd fainted, and another nurse wheeled her to the waiting area and parked her next to my chair. Bobbi had managed to remain mostly calm while she'd filled out forms and handed over her insurance card, but I sensed her angst building again.

She sat with her face in one hand and a wad of tissues in the other.

"Bobbi," I said gently. "Let me call your daughter for you. Alisha, right? I'm sure she'd want to be here."

Bobbi shook her head. "This will only worry her. She has her studies to think about. An important test coming up."

"I know, but did you consider that maybe she has a right to worry? You are her mom, and she needs to know what happened."

She sniffed and shook her head. "I'm sure I'm fine. There's no need to bother her."

I thought about the relationship between me and my mother. I would be angry if something like this happened, and she didn't tell me. Not to mention, someone should keep an eye on Bobbi for the next little while. "Still, she's going to hear about Karyn. There will be no helping that. Give her the chance to know that you're being looked after so that she doesn't have to wonder if you're okay, too."

I knew I was rambling, but I'd made valid points.

When Bobbi hesitated to answer, I wondered if I'd gotten past the first hurdle. "Let me call her, okay? You need her with you."

Her expression wavered, and I pressed harder. "What's her number?"

Instead of arguing, Bobbi dropped her head in defeat and told me Alisha's number. I waited until the nurse arrived to claim Bobbi and wheel her away before I called her daughter.

Ten minutes later, Alisha Knowles walked in. Another young woman with glossy, nut brown hair strode beside her, and they stopped at the reception desk. The woman behind the counter pointed in my direction, and I stood.

Alisha Knowles and her friend hurried toward me. Bobbi's daughter was a natural beauty, with long blond hair and green eyes. She shared many of her mother's facial features, looking like a younger, healthier version of Bobbi.

She swallowed when she stopped in front of me. "You're Daisy? The one who called?"

I gave her a reassuring smile. "I am. Let's sit."

Alisha released a shaky breath as they both sat. "Is my mom okay?"

I nodded. "I think she'll be fine. She received some really bad news this evening. It was enough of a jolt that she fainted."

Alisha inhaled sharply and put a hand over her mouth, the same as her mother had done. "That's bad."

No doubt about that. "Does she do that often? Faint?"

Alisha quickly shook her head. "No. Never."

I sent her and her friend what I hoped was a comforting smile. "Well, that's why we're here. To make sure she's okay otherwise. But I truly think she'll be fine. She woke up before the paramedics had arrived, and though she's been upset, she seems pretty stable."

The dark-haired girl next to her wrapped an arm around Alisha's shoulders. "Try not to worry, Al. I'm sure she's okay."

Alisha's friend focused on me. "What awful thing happened?"

I groaned inwardly, wishing someone else had been chosen as the bearer of troubling news. I turned to face Alisha who looked at me with trepidation in her eyes. "You know her friend Karyn, right?"

Alisha glanced at her friend and back to me before she nodded.

I exhaled a slow breath. "Karyn died tonight."

The dark-haired girl inhaled a sharp breath, looking as though someone had stabbed her in the heart. Then she released a wail that pierced my soul. *"No!"*

She stood to face me and then crumpled to the floor as she struggled to breathe.

Disbelief flooded me as I studied the dark-haired girl's features closer. Then horror washed in. "Oh, no. That's not..."

The girl's raspy, panicked breaths and wide eyes alarmed me.

Alisha cried out and dropped to the floor next to her.

My insides tightened into fierce, painful knots. "We need help," I called out and then knelt next to the two girls.

Alisha had begun to cry as she tried to calm her friend. "Sailor. *Sailor.*" She stroked her cheek. "Just breathe."

I rhythmically patted Sailor's shoulder hoping that would give her something to focus on. "Everything's going to be okay, honey. Try to take a deeper breath."

Alisha glanced at me as if I was the monster that I felt like. "Karyn is her *mom*," she accused.

I shook my head and searched for any words that would remotely be acceptable. "I'm so sorry. I...I didn't recognize her. I thought her hair was blond like yours."

Alisha jerked her gaze toward the reception desk and yelled for help again, even though a nurse in bright pink scrubs was hurrying toward us.

The woman dropped to the floor next to Sailor. She lifted her hand and placed two fingers on her wrist. "What happened?"

I swallowed the bile in my throat. "She's hyperventilating. I inadvertently told her that her mom died tonight. I wasn't aware of her identity, or I wouldn't have said anything."

The nurse flashed me a look that questioned my intelligence. I didn't blame her. I'd literally delivered shocking news to two people that night which had caused them to have medical issues.

"She has asthma," Alisha offered.

The nurse tilted Sailor's face toward her. "I know what you're feeling is frightening. But you're safe. Try not to panic. We're going to help you, okay?"

Sailor shook her head and continued to struggle.

A younger male nurse rushed toward us, pushing a wheelchair.

The female nurse nodded at him. "Let's get her off the floor."

The two professionals placed Sailor into the wheelchair and then the older woman wheeled her away with quickened footsteps.

The young man looked at Alisha. "You are?"

Tears fell from Alisha's eyes as she got to her feet. "I'm her friend. Please let me go with her. Her mom died tonight, and I'm not sure where her dad is. My mom's here somewhere, too. Everything is so messed up. I can't even..."

The tone of Alisha's voice made me fear that she was close to entering a state of utter panic, too.

He gestured in the direction that Sailor had been taken. "Go. Catch up to them."

Alisha scurried away.

Then he looked at me with questioning eyes.

I shook my head. "Just a bystander who tried to help." And failed miserably.

He gave me a nod of approval. "I'm sure they appreciated it."

He left me sitting there and returned to the front desk. Others in the after-hours care watched me with suspicion, as though they knew the truth, and uncomfortable heat rushed across my cheeks.

I gathered Corey's coat and headed for the exit, needing fresh air to clear my head and soothe my spirit. And I needed my feet on firm ground after the tragedy that had befallen our town that night.

FOUR

I would have gone home after the disaster at the medical center if my conscience would have allowed it. The Goddess knew I needed a hug and consoling words from Gideon, not to mention snuggles from my kitties, but I had another stop to make first.

In trying to help Bobbi, I'd created multiple disasters, and I needed to do as much damage control as I could without making things worse. If that was even possible at this point.

The drive back to the fitness studio seemed quicker than it had earlier. Maybe because I was dreading what awaited me. I parked in the same spot as I had before and headed for the entrance. Young Officer Eaton who'd been chided before by Corey had been assigned to door duty, it seemed.

Poor guy. He was having a bad night, too. I lifted a hand in greeting as I approached.

He frowned. "I'm sorry, ma'am. I can't let you enter. As you can see from the yellow tape, this is a crime scene."

I did my best to smile. "Yes, I know. I was here earlier, remember?"

He barely looked at me before he shook his head. "My commanding officer said not to let anyone enter."

I released my exasperation with a sigh, knowing that he was trying to follow his boss's exact instructions. "Corey is the one I need to speak to. Could you let him know that I'm here?"

The young man shook his head. "I would suggest going to his office tomorrow morning. That would be a better time."

My sympathy for the inept officer quickly waned. "I need to talk to him now. This can't wait."

He shifted his stance and glared at me this time. "Ma'am. Please do what I ask."

I snorted. "Or what? You'll arrest me?"

He narrowed his gaze. "That's up to you. I would suggest complying with my request."

I stared at him, giving him one last chance to see reason. He only blinked.

"Fine," I said and stepped back until I was well away from his precious crime scene tape. Then I pulled out my phone and dialed Corey's number.

It took several rings before he answered. "Daisy? Everything okay?"

The sound of his voice, warm and caring, churned the aftereffects of the evening inside me, and my throat tightened. "Not exactly. I need to speak to you about tonight."

He hesitated for a moment. "You know I'm in the middle of an investigation."

A shiver started in my core and radiated outward. "Yes. This is important. I promise."

He sighed. "Fine. We need to get your statement anyway. Can you come back?"

I focused on the cop in front of me and caught a nervous tick at the side of his eye. "I'm already here, but your officer won't let me in."

"Tell him I said it's okay."

I exhaled my frustration and held the phone away from my ear. "Corey says it's okay if I go inside."

Officer Eaton narrowed his gaze in suspicion. "How do I know that's who you're talking to?"

Corey must have heard his response because a growl of irritation echoed from my phone, and I raised my brows.

A few seconds later, the door of the studio swung open, and Corey focused on his man. "Let her in."

The young officer visibly swallowed. "Yes, sir."

I hated to make the guy's life harder, but he seemed plenty competent to do that on his own. He didn't look at me as I lifted the yellow tape and walked beneath it.

Corey rolled his eyes as I approached though he didn't comment. He stopped just inside the door and met my gaze. "What's up?"

I bit my bottom lip, thrust his jacket toward him, and wished I could hide in a hole. "I screwed up. Big time."

He absentmindedly accepted the jacket he'd loaned to Bobbi as he searched my eyes. "How?"

I rubbed the middle of my forehead where a dull ache had set in. "Well, besides causing Bobbi to faint, I also inadvertently told Sailor Strickland that her mother was dead."

He stared at me for a long moment and then sighed. "Care to explain how that happened?"

I dropped my shoulders as defeat set in. "At the clinic, I insisted that Bobbi let me call her daughter. Alisha arrived not long after with a friend, and Alisha needed to know what had happened to Bobbi, so I told her. But I didn't realize the girl with her was Karyn's daughter. I thought Sailor had long blond hair, like Alisha. But it's brown now, and I never would have said anything if I'd known. Alisha deserved to hear the news from you or someone who knows her, not a random stranger who seems to be quite capable of messing everything up, and then Sailor started hyperventilating. Alisha was crying. The nurse had to come and—"

Corey placed his hands on my upper arms. "Whoa, whoa. Take it easy."

The concern he showed me brought my emotions to the surface, and I blinked back tears. But as hard as I tried, that didn't stop them from flowing.

Corey widened his eyes as though he didn't know what to do, and then he pulled me in for a hug.

I probably shouldn't have let him, knowing the way he felt about me, but I didn't stop him. I soaked up the reassuring energy he offered and then pulled away, inhaling a shuddering breath. "I'm so sorry. I feel horrible about blurting the news."

He tipped his head from side to side as though weighing my news. "I agree that it's not optimal. Is Sailor okay?"

I wiped tears from beneath my eyes. "I don't really know. A nurse took her to an exam room, to give her a breathing treatment, I think. She has asthma."

He nodded and sighed. "Well, this probably sounds crass, but telling her is one less thing on my list. Though I should contact Sailor's dad to let him know. Sailor will need some support in the coming days."

I nodded, still feeling terrible.

He lifted his chin as though encouraging me. "It's an awful situation, but it's not your fault. Sailor would have heard the news tonight, either way, and probably would have reacted the same. If so, she was lucky to be at the clinic where they could help her."

His words brought a small amount of peace to my soul, though I was still upset by what had happened. "I suppose."

He thumbed toward the hallway. "Let's sit for a minute, and you can tell me what you remember, okay?"

I really wanted to go home, but telling him everything first meant I wouldn't have to go to the station tomorrow. I could say my piece and go home. "Yeah. Sure."

He led me to an office not far from Karyn's, and I could hear police personnel talking as they processed the crime scene. I was fairly certain they wouldn't have moved the body yet, and I opened my senses to see if Karyn's spirit had remained.

Nothing stood out, and I was relieved.

Helping a spirit pass to the other side had been an amazing experience for me, but I wasn't ready to tackle another just yet.

I claimed one of the light brown rattan chairs and was surprised when Corey sat in the one next to me instead of across the desk. Maybe he'd done so because we weren't in his office.

He pulled a small notebook from his pocket and opened it. "Tell me everything you can remember."

I relaxed against the back of the chair, knowing a hot bath and a glass of wine waited for me at home. "I'm probably not much help, but here goes. Nicole convinced me to come to her exercise class. Part way through, we took a break, and that's when I noticed Liza who'd come in to talk to Karyn. From where I sat across the room, they seemed to be having a heated discussion."

I paused to give him a chance to catch up with his note-taking. When he lifted his gaze, I continued. "Right after class, I went to the front to fill my water bottle. On my way back, I caught a man and a woman down a darkened hallway kissing. I only mention it because they acted odd, like they were strangers instead of comforting each other when we were all in the studio for questioning."

He raised his brow. "Who was this?"

I moistened my dry lips. "Liza and the guy that Officer Kemp brought in."

Corey nodded as he took notes. "Justin Hancock. That's interesting. Kemp told me he was Karyn's boyfriend."

I lifted my brows. "If that's the case, then that doesn't look good for either one of them."

He finished writing and looked at me. "No, it doesn't. What else do you have for me?"

I inhaled and prepared to finish my story. "After that, I headed for the shower. When I got out, most of the class had gone. Tamra Church was still in the locker room, though she took one look at me and hurried off."

He scratched above his eyebrow. "Any idea why?"

I shook my head. "No. She's always been somewhat socially awkward though."

"I'll have someone track her down for a statement."

I nodded. "Then it was just after I finished dressing that I heard an awful scream. In the hall, I followed the sounds of a woman crying and found Liza in that office. She had a phone in her hand and had called you guys. She screamed when she saw me and dropped the resistance band she'd been holding. At first, I didn't see the body because it was hidden behind the desk. But then I looked, and Karyn was obviously dead. Strangled, I think. Maybe with that resistance band."

He narrowed his gaze. "Liza didn't mention the band in her statement."

I shrugged. "Maybe she forgot? She was pretty distraught."

He studied me, but didn't agree or disagree. "So, Liza called for help. Not you?"

"She did."

He tapped the pen on his notebook. "A couple of things. I'm concerned about the kiss and that band. We've already taken Justin's statement and let him go because he said he was at the other end of the studio, wearing headphones while he lifted weights. Said he didn't hear or see anything."

It was my turn to lift my brows. "Did he seem credible?"

Corey pointed his pen in my direction. "I didn't interview him, but I'll have an officer round him up and take him to the station for further questioning."

I tapped my finger on the desk, but stopped when I realized I was copying Corey's actions. "You know, Bobbi said she was also wearing headphones and didn't hear the screams."

He narrowed his gaze thoughtfully. "I supposed that's not uncommon, but it's worth noting."

I glanced at my watch, expecting I could be out of there in five minutes or less. "One more thing Bobbi told me. I asked if she knew anyone who might want to hurt Karyn. She mentioned Liza, said that they hadn't been getting along, but when I pressed her, she didn't know why."

He met my gaze and snorted. "Another thing Liza failed to mention."

He stood abruptly and headed for the office door. "Luckily, Liza is still here, and we can ask her right now."

FIVE

As Corey headed for the office door, I stood and held up a hand to stop him, but he disappeared without noticing. I glanced at the notebook and pen he'd left on the desk and decided that he likely meant to bring Liza into the office to question her. But he surely wouldn't want me in on the interview. Would he?

I decided he wouldn't. My job was done, and I could leave.

The moment I stepped into the hall, though, Corey called my name. He strode toward me with Liza next to him. "Don't leave just yet, Daisy."

My insides turned to mush, and I cringed. As much as I wanted to know what Liza would say, I'd rather skip the drama and have Corey tell me later.

Corey ushered us inside, and I dropped onto my original chair. This time he sat across the desk, and Liza timidly claimed the one next to me. Her eyes were swollen and redder than when I'd left earlier, and the energy she radiated was almost non-existent. I had to wonder what had taken place during Sofia's interview.

Liza met my gaze. "Corey said you had something to tell me."

I nearly keeled over. "He what?" I stuttered.

Corey nodded at me. "I'd like you to tell her what you saw when you went to the water fountain and also what Bobbi said about her and Karyn."

I looked at him aghast. "Can't you?"

He opened his hand, encouraging me. "You witnessed it."

I swallowed, certain Corey was not using customary police tactics. "Okay, then. Right after class, I saw you in the hallway with Justin."

Any color that remained in her face, blanched. She stared at me but didn't speak.

"You were kissing Karyn's boyfriend," I added. I had no idea if Karyn and Justin had been a couple, but Corey wasn't the type to get his information wrong. I figured I might as well toss it out there so that I could be done and go home.

Liza quickly shook her head. "No, you misunderstood."

I snorted. "Pretty sure I didn't. He had his arms around you, and your mouths were together. I don't know how I could construe that as anything else."

Corey focused on Liza. "You might as well tell the truth. It will come out sooner or later. Were you and Justin having an affair behind Karyn's back?"

She glanced toward the doorway, and I sensed her desperation. "It's...it's not what you think."

Corey nodded. "Then tell me what it is."

Liza buried her face in her hand. "It was nothing. Just a kiss."

She looked at us, her eyelashes wet with tears. "We never slept together. We didn't. I just...something was wrong with Karyn. She'd been so awful lately. I was supposed to be her best friend, and she treated me like garbage. Everyone, really."

I lifted my brows. "And you thought starting something with her boyfriend would fix that?"

She quickly shook her head. "No. Of course not. Just...it was dumb, okay? I was hurt and angry, so one day, I flirted with Justin. I just teased him a little. The next day, he flirted back. It was harmless. Sometimes, Karyn was even in the room. You can flirt with someone and not have it mean anything."

I widened my eyes in disbelief. I would never act that way with my friends' significant others. "But you did more than flirt."

She waved away my comment. "Tonight was the first time. And he kissed me."

"You didn't look like you were protesting."

Corey nodded, approving of my questioning, and I frowned at him. I wasn't the investigator here. He was.

Liza wiped more tears from her cheeks. "He caught me by surprise, okay? And it was...nice. But it only lasted a few seconds."

"That doesn't make it okay," I challenged.

Liza glared at me. "Haven't you ever found yourself in an unexpected situation, caught off guard by someone's actions, and needed a moment to process and react?"

Truth be told, I was in that exact situation at the moment. But I'd like to think I'd acted honorably. I met her gaze head-on. "If one of my friends' husband or boyfriend kissed me, I'd slap his face."

She shook her head and looked away. "We can't all be as perfect as you, Daisy Summers."

I frowned. I was far from perfect, but I wasn't a jerk where my friends were concerned.

Corey cleared his throat. "Bobbi also confided in Daisy, saying that you and Karyn had been at odds with each other lately."

Liza glared at Corey, and the meekness she'd shown when she'd first walked in had been replaced with a feisty attitude. "I already told you that Karyn was being awful to everyone. It wasn't just me."

Corey adjusted the ball cap on his head. "Anyone you'd care to name?"

She snorted. "Bobbi for starters. She's not as sweet as you might think. Karyn's daughter for another. Her ex-husband. Justin. Pretty much everyone she knew."

Corey jotted in his notebook and then lifted his gaze. "Any idea what was up with Karyn? Why the sudden change in her manner?"

Liza shook her head in frustration. "If we'd been as good of friends as I'd once thought, she might have confided in me. But she didn't."

Corey studied her for a long moment, and Liza glanced between the two of us. "Is that all? I have a beast of a headache. So, unless you're going to arrest me, I'd like to go home."

Corey hesitated and then sighed. "You're free to go. For now."

Liza jumped from her seat and headed for the door.

"Don't leave town," Corey called after her.

The energy in the room grew still and quiet. But not the fury inside me. *"What was that?"*

He sent me a puzzled expression. "What?"

I opened my hands wide. "You. Throwing me under the bus, making me confront Liza."

He gave a soft snort and smiled. "Sorry about that. I needed to force her hand, and you were the best way to do that. I apologize if you weren't up for the task."

I wrinkled my nose. "Task? I'm not one of your employees."

He lifted his hands in surrender. "Sorry. I'm not trying to make things worse here. With the way you've talked to suspects and searched out information in the past, I thought you might like the chance to officially question her."

I grew uncomfortable and shifted in my seat. "I don't question suspects."

He snorted a laugh. "Really? So, what was the point in asking Bobbi her thoughts on who might want to harm Karyn?"

I opened my mouth to speak and then shut it. He was right. That was exactly what I'd done. I huffed. "Are we done here? Because I also have a beast of a headache, and I'd like to go home, too."

He sent me a gentle smile as he stood. "Come on. I'll walk you out."

Officer Eaton kept his gaze focused on something in the distance as we exited the building. At my car, Corey opened the door for me but lightly gripped me by the elbow before I could enter. I lifted my gaze to him in question.

He searched my face and then focused on my eyes. "I just want to make sure you're okay. That we're okay. I know tonight has been a lot, and I shouldn't have put you on the spot."

Sincerity radiated from him, and any lingering irritation I might have had floated away. "It's fine. I'm fine."

A hint of a smile touched the corner of his lips. "You have something I don't, and I envy that."

His words perplexed me. "Envy what? My magic?"

He gave a brief nod. "Your ability to read people, to push them when they need pushing. I'm good at my job, but I know Liza wouldn't have said what she did if you hadn't been there."

I blushed at his compliment. "I'm sure you would have done fine."

His gaze grew thoughtful and then he focused on me. "But it's easier with you around."

I hadn't expected this from him, and it left my thoughts spinning. "Thank you. I appreciate that."

He dipped his head in acceptance. "Anytime. Drive safe, okay?"

I had the urge to reach out and connect with him. Touch his hand or his face, but I refrained. "Always. Have a good night."

He stared into my eyes, and the connection warmed my heart. "You, too."

He waited until I was seated before he closed the door between us, gave me a small wave, and headed back to the Expanding Universe for what I knew would be a long night's work.

I started my car but didn't put it into drive. Instead, I replayed what he'd said about my skills. Reading people had always come easy to me, to most empaths, but maybe I had something extra. Maybe that's why I couldn't seem to leave a mystery unsolved, why questions gnawed at me until I had answers.

I glanced toward the building, thought of Corey again, and shook my head. I wished I knew what to do with him. If Gideon hadn't been in my life, I was sure I'd give the guy a chance. I'd certainly been interested in him when I was younger. Corey was handsome, kind, and the nervousness I'd once felt around him had faded.

But I had Gideon now, and though my mind might wonder about Corey, the charming demon was the one who'd stolen my heart.

I wondered if perhaps, I should be grateful for Corey's friendship and let things be just that. Friends.

It seemed like the best solution.

With that decision made, I slipped my car's gear into drive and headed toward the home that had become my sanctuary. Gideon was always good to help me sort through my feelings and ease my stress, which was exactly what I needed.

SIX

I woke up the next morning feeling hungover. Gideon hadn't been home when I'd arrived the night before. The quick message he'd left on the table said he'd been called away and hoped he wouldn't be gone for long.

I was sad that he hadn't made it home by the time I'd finished two glasses of wine and had soaked forever in a warm, bubbly tub. But I was certain I'd reached a point of relaxation and could sleep.

Of course, the second my head hit the pillow, a myriad of thoughts came alive and tumbled through my mind. About Gideon. About Corey. And another murder in my hometown.

I wasn't sure how many hours had passed before I'd finally drifted off. All I knew was that Gideon hadn't come home before then.

As I prepared to go to work and dressed in my brown and pink Meowkins t-shirt, a memory, or perhaps a dream, of Gideon kissing the top of my head while I'd slept filtered in. I wondered if he'd come into my room after he'd returned, but I couldn't be certain.

I did, however, peek into his room to ensure that he'd made it home the previous night. He lay sleeping with one arm over his head, and my two kitties snuggled up near him. Freya lifted her head to look at me, but then she sighed and curled into a tighter ball.

I wished I had the capability of communicating with Freya, like the high priestess of my coven Jocelyn did with her gorgeous black cat, Raven. Since the previous night and my plans to sit down with

Freya to practice hadn't worked out like I'd expected, I committed to trying again that night.

If Jocelyn could do it, I could.

The morning at Meowkins was average. One of my favorite customers, Gilbert, came in with his wife, Ellen, and the two of them always made me smile. In the past, Gilbert had usually come alone, but recently, Ellen had begun to join him, which made my heart happy.

Not to mention, Ellen loved a fresh cappuccino, and she giggled every time she ordered one of my signature Cat-puccinos, complete with paw-print foam.

The café quieted from the morning rush, and Nicole emerged from the Purry Parlor where we housed cats from our local shelter, hoping to give them more exposure and help them find homes. She untied the apron she used in the parlor and hung it on a hook near the hall leading into the backroom. "I need more coffee. The last shot of caffeine wasn't enough."

Aeri twisted from the back counter, her straight dark hair brushing the tops of her shoulders as she did. "Because of Karyn's death?"

Murder, I wanted to say and correct her because I was certain that's what had happened to Karyn. But I hadn't settled from the previous night's drama and didn't want more.

Nicole paused to wash her hands and pumped soap from the dispenser. "Mostly Karyn."

The event had weighed heavily on us both. "Mostly? I hope you weren't fighting with Cliff again."

She gave us a casual shrug. "No. We barely talked last night."

I met Aeri's gaze, and she mirrored mine of concern. We both knew that regularly not talking to your significant other was never a good sign. Still, I'd try to be positive for Nicole's sake. "I guess that's better than fighting."

She sighed and suddenly seemed more tired. "Not really. It just means that I'm no longer bugging him for attention. He's happy to watch television and go to bed early. I didn't even bother telling him what had happened to Karyn."

I widened my eyes and nodded. I wouldn't repeat the speech I'd given her a million times letting her know that she deserved love, support, and attention from Cliff. She knew, and I knew, and hopefully one day, she'd do something about it.

My sweet friend exhaled her frustration. "Look, I know it's not the best situation, and I would never consider marrying him." She snorted. "If he'd even ever ask, but it is what it is right now."

My senses jumped to attention, and I studied Nicole closer. "Right now? That sounds like it might have an end date."

Aeri moved closer until she stood next to me. "Are the winds of change shifting?"

Nicole rolled her eyes. "I don't know. Maybe."

Despite her tiredness and frustration, I detected a hint of something else. "What did you end up doing to distract yourself?"

Her gaze flicked to me fast enough to confirm my suspicion. "I watched a movie."

"At home?" I pressed.

She glanced at me from the corner of her eye as she squeezed between us to grab a coffee cup. "Yes, at home."

Aeri questioned me with a look, and I gave her a hopeful smile. "Alone?" I asked.

Nicole finished pouring her coffee and lifted her gaze. "Do you think I'm crazy enough to invite someone over?"

The fact that she didn't outright confirm that she'd been alone left me to wonder. She'd mentioned before that she and her sister who lived in Montana sometimes shared a screen and watched movies together, messaging on their phones with each other as they did. "No, but you might have watched with someone virtually."

Her face flushed bright red. "Using your talents against me isn't nice, Daisy."

Her accusation dimmed the excitement I'd felt from chasing down leads regarding her love life. "I'm sorry. I just want what's best for you. You know that."

Aeri lifted a hand and wiggled her finger. "Uh, no. Don't fall for that, Daisy. Don't let her guilt you. Nicole's our best friend, and if she's watching movies with someone besides her sister, I want to know."

Nicole groaned. "Fine. I watched the movie with Rory."

Aeri widened her eyes the color of brownies into large ovals. "What, girlfriend? You have a man on the side?"

I laughed even as Nicole cringed. "Don't say it like that. We're just friends hanging out."

"Uh-huh," I teased. "I know that line. Might have used it a time or two myself."

She shook her head quickly. "Don't read too much into it. Honestly, we *are* just friends who like talking to each other. I won't stay with Cliff if that ever changes, okay?"

Aeri chuckled. "And you'll tell us, right?"

Nicole narrowed her gaze in a teasing gesture at Aeri. "You'll be the first to know."

Aeri threw an arm across Nicole's shoulders and hugged her. "I hope it's sooner than later," she whispered.

Nicole sipped her coffee. "I'd rather talk about something else."

Aeri turned to me. "Like who had it in for poor Karyn. Nicole seems to think it might be Liza."

That would be my first guess. "She did have the means and opportunity."

Nicole gestured with her coffee cup. "I've wondered if Justin helped in some way. After all, you did find them together."

I frowned. "I don't know. I mean, maybe. But what would be the point? Karyn and Justin weren't married. Justin could easily walk away at any time and take up with Liza instead. Karyn would be angry, no doubt, but I don't think that justifies murder, do you?"

Aeri shook her head.

Nicole paused for a moment and then agreed. "You'll let us know what you find out, though, right?"

I opened my hands in question. "What do you mean?"

Aeri lifted her shoulder in a half shrug. "Aren't you going to poke around a little? Like you've done before? You seem to enjoy it."

They had noticed, too. "I can't help that this kind of thing interests me, and the need for justice burns strong. But I've had other things on my mind lately. Like introducing Gideon to my mom."

Nicole grinned. "For as long as I've known you, righting the wrongs of the universe has always meant something to you. I guess you never had the opportunity to explore that curiosity beyond your own small world before."

Her words stunned me. I hadn't. I'd kept my circle so small, my life so controlled, that I rarely paid attention to anything beyond that.

I'd missed out, I realized. Missed out on much of life. Not just the investigations, but having conversations with people beyond saying good morning and wishing them a good day.

Since my life had been upended, I'd helped people. Helped bring about justice. Helped a poor, tortured soul find his way to peace. "I suppose that's true."

Aeri studied me. "Things have changed for you, Daisy, in case you haven't noticed. Your world has grown. You've grown, and it's a good look on you. You're amazing at seeing details. I'm not certain the other murders would have been solved without your excellent perception skills."

Nicole nodded in agreement.

I drew my brows together and then filled my own coffee cup. "You act like I'm suddenly so much better at reading people than I was before."

Nicole turned to Aeri who turned to me. "You really haven't noticed?"

I lifted a hand. "Okay. Stop. Don't make me out to be something I'm not. Justice interests me, but Corey is strong and smart and more than capable of handling things. He doesn't need me."

Nicole tilted her head. "Strong, smart, and capable. All that's missing is handsome, and we all know he's that and more."

Aeri grabbed two packets of sugar and passed them to me. "Are you reconsidering another date with him?"

I scrunched my features into an annoyed look. "Why would you even ask that?"

She shrugged. "I don't know. You mentioned Corey multiple times this morning when you were telling me about what went down last night."

"Because he was the top officer investigating the crime scene. It's hard not to include him."

Aeri sent me a dubious look. "It was the way you talked about him. Also, he was the one who investigated the last two cases that you were involved with, and you barely mentioned him."

I considered her suggestion and then shook my head. "No. The previous two times, I wasn't there when the murders occurred. This time I was. Plus, Bobbi gave me information that Corey needed to know, not to mention, I had to tell him about my screw up with Sailor."

I glanced between my two friends thinking I was the one who now wanted to change the subject. "I don't suppose you talked to anyone this morning who mentioned how Bobbi or Sailor is doing."

They both shook their heads. "You know," Aeri said. "Even though you don't want to be a part of this, you kind of are, and I think you're going to worry until you find out how they're doing."

She was right. "Probably, but I'll just call Corey. He can tell me."

Aeri snorted. "If you think that's the best, then okay. Let us know what you hear."

Instead of answering her, I met her gaze over the rim of my cup and sipped my coffee. I wasn't sure where all their wild ideas were coming from, but I hadn't changed my mind about Gideon and had suddenly become interested in Corey instead. And my powers of perception were the same as they'd always been. I just didn't have as much to perceive before.

A customer entered the café, and Aeri deserted our conversation to help the older woman.

Nicole gave me a hopeful look. "At least tell me you'll still be my workout buddy. It was so fun with you there."

I snorted. "Didn't our teacher just die?"

She nodded. "Yeah, but they're moving forward. I got an email this morning. Karyn's class will be temporarily postponed until they find a new teacher, but the weight room is open and yoga classes will resume tomorrow."

I drew my brows in confusion. "Doesn't Liza teach those?"

Nicole shrugged. "Yep."

I had a hard time finding much to admire about the woman. "And she's back at work already? As if she didn't just lose her so-called best friend?"

"It seems so. But, you know, people handle grief differently. Some need to work to get their mind off things."

"Maybe so. But this wasn't a regular death, and Karyn died at that studio. How could Liza possibly focus and feel well enough to teach a class?"

Nicole lifted a teasing brow. "You could join me and find out."

I truly wished I could decline, but I yearned to see Liza's demeanor for myself. "Fine. But only for yoga from now on."

After all, how hard could sitting on a mat or kneeling be?

SEVEN

I'd just finished serving coffee to two businessmen when a tingle of awareness raised goosebumps on my skin. I looked up to find Gideon strolling into the coffee shop carrying Freya in one arm and Old Grey's carrier in the other hand.

I loved the way Gideon's loose cotton shirt and faded jeans gave him a breezy, confident appearance, but it was his eyes that always hit me the hardest. When his gaze met mine and sparkled with genuine happiness, my heart melted. "Hey, my lovely. The kits and I decided to hang out with you for the morning."

The kits, I thought with a chuckle. "That's a nice surprise. Give me a minute, and I'll meet you in the Purry Parlor. I'll introduce you to the newest addition to our café."

My best friend Aeri sidled up next to me with a grin on her face. "Good morning, Gideon. It's good to see you."

He dipped his head in greeting. "Lovely Aeri, it's nice to see you as well." Then he gestured toward the parlor. "Nicole is here?"

I nodded.

He grinned. "Wonderful. I'll chat with her."

Aeri turned her dark brown eyes full of mischief in my direction and tucked a strand of her silky black hair behind one ear. "The kits? It almost sounded like he said the kids."

I snorted. "Even if Gideon and I do take our relationship to the next level, there will never be kids. Only kitties."

She gave me a knowing look. "I get it. There's no way I'll be having more kids at this age, either. Two is enough."

"Yes, well, you're lucky because the two that you have are perfect."

Aeri rolled her eyes. "That's a lie, and you know it. You babysat for me a few times years ago. You know how they can be."

I thought of her twin boys with their mischievous dark eyes and quick smiles. "Still, they're as perfect as any two rambunctious teenage boys can be."

She grinned, unable to hide how proud she was of them. "Okay. I'll accept that. Now, get in there with your man. I've got this covered."

I finished washing a silver milk frothing pitcher and set it aside to dry. Then I leaned close to my friend. "I won't be too long. I didn't get a chance to talk to him last night about Karyn, and I'm sure he has questions."

She widened her eyes in agreement. "Don't we all?"

Nicole sat on a rug with Gideon, chatting happily as nearly a dozen cats available for adoption surrounded them, sniffing Gideon or vying for space on their laps. I grinned as I entered. "Looks like you two have your hands full."

Nicole pointed to Gideon. "His fault. Every time he comes in, they all race to see him."

Gideon glanced sideways up at me and quirked his mouth into a grin. "I'm a cat magnet. What can I say?"

He scooped up the gorgeous Siamese who'd recently come to stay at my cat sanctuary. "Look at this beautiful girl. Nooni."

I approached and sat on the floor next to Gideon, my knee bumping his. "I see that you've already met. Nooni, huh? I suppose that's a cute name."

I reached over and scratched the little lady's forehead. She closed her pretty blue eyes until they were slits, and her purrs grew louder.

Gideon turned the cat to face him. "Tell her that you picked your name, not me."

Nicole chuckled. "Is speaking to cats a new skill you've acquired?"

He lifted his brow and regarded her. "It's not a new skill. I've been adept in feline communication for a while now."

I frowned at him. "Adept? I knew you had some ability, but I didn't know you were proficient."

His eyes twinkled. "Perhaps there are other things you've yet to learn about me, as well."

I smiled at his sassiness. "I could say the same."

He widened his eyes in interest. "Oh, yes. I am looking forward to learning more."

Nicole sat Oliver, the sand-colored tabby she'd been holding, to the side. "It's getting a little too steamy in here for me. I think I need an iced coffee."

Gideon laughed, the sound warm and rich. "Sorry, Nicole. I tend to lose my sensibilities when I'm around this lovely lady."

Nicole glanced at each of us. "You guys want anything?"

We both declined with shakes of our heads.

Though I loved every bit of his flirtations, I regarded him with a suspicious look. "The charm is oozing from you this morning. What's up?"

He drew his brows down in a wounded look. "Does something have to be up for me to let you know I'm fascinated by you?"

I studied him for a long moment. "No, but I can tell there's something you're not saying."

Gideon finally conceded with a nod. "The downside of getting close to a person."

"What do you mean?"

He wiggled a finger between the two of us. "The more time we spend together, the stronger our connection grows. You picked up on my unspoken thoughts."

I tilted my head, trying to read his emotions. "Is allowing me to get closer something that you regret, then?"

He reassured me with a firm shake of his head. "Never."

I paused for a moment to string his statements together. "So, what you're basically saying is that I'm now able to read you better, which also means that I was right. There's something else going on."

He chuckled. "The art of distraction has never worked well with you."

I narrowed my eyes. "And yet, here you are avoiding the subject once again."

He dropped his gaze to Nooni who sat contentedly in his lap, and he began to stroke her light tan fur and black face. "I didn't want you to be angry because I didn't make it home until very late last night."

His confession brought a smile to my face. "I'm not your keeper, Gideon. You're free to come and go as you please. I'm the one living in your house, remember?"

He focused on me, and the slightest flash of black darkened his eyes, giving me a shiver. "Oh, aye. I'm well aware of our living situation, of how it feels to have you near."

The tension between us had thickened, causing my heart to flutter in a wild but not unwelcome way. I swallowed, trying to moisten my suddenly dry throat. "I'm not angry with you, Gideon. I'll admit that I would have loved a big hug from you after my awful day, but I know you have other things in your life besides me."

He reached over and drew a thumb down my cheek. "There's nothing more important than you."

Goddess help me, the man had a way with words, and he seemed to have no problem whatsoever expressing his feelings. Unlike me. "Did you want me to be angry with you?"

He held my gaze and softly shook his head. "No, of course not. But I wouldn't mind if you cared to know what kept me away until the wee morning hours."

Clarity drifted in like the passing of a morning mist. "Oh. I see."

I paused, trying to formulate my question into words. "I *was* worried about you. I always am when you're away. I know that you deal with very powerful people who might not have the same kind heart that you do, and that frightens me a little."

Or a lot.

He inched closer until the full length of his thigh touched mine, and he wrapped an arm around me. "Do not fear for me, Daisy. I'm quite competent with my skills."

A shiver rolled through me, bringing to light exactly how much I'd worried about him. "Even though I don't know what most of those skills are, I'm sure that you are."

"But?" he prompted.

I met his gaze. "But that rogue demon is still out there, and I can tell by the way that you talk about him that he's dangerous."

Gideon nodded thoughtfully. "And you think he might be stronger than me because I haven't caught him yet."

I widened my eyes in question but didn't speak.

He tugged my head close to his and kissed my hair. "He's young and foolish, Daisy. But he won't escape his consequences forever. And I have yet to use everything in my arsenal."

The threat remained in the air around us, and I wished I dared to ask what his weapons or his plans might be. Instead, I nodded in understanding.

He exhaled a deep breath and curved his lips into a small smile. "I do apologize, my lovely, for causing you worry and for not being here for you when you needed me."

I shrugged. "It's okay. I managed like I always do."

He nodded. "You accepted solace from another."

I drew my brows in question.

He cautiously met my gaze. "From Corey Shelton."

My insides tightened into an uncomfortable knot. "Corey? Yeah, I guess he did give me a brief hug when I was upset, but I wouldn't exactly call it taking solace from him."

I knew Gideon had the ability to see me, see what I was doing, whenever he chose to. After all, I'd agreed to let him keep a photo of the two of us on his phone that would allow him to check on me if I experienced any kind of alarm. "Since you were watching me then, you should have seen that it was an innocent hug."

"I wasn't watching. I do try to respect your privacy. It was that I smelled his cologne on your hair when I checked on you early this morning."

That meant I hadn't imagined him coming into my room. "You could smell his cologne when we'd only briefly touched?"

He shrugged. "My senses are heightened. More so where you're concerned. I can't help it."

This was news, and I felt bad that I'd caused him to worry about our relationship. "I...I'm sorry?" I offered in a half-hearted apology. "I inadvertently did a couple of things that hurt people last night, and I was upset. He was only trying to help me feel better. Honestly, if you'd give him a chance, you'd see that he's a good guy."

A sly smile crossed Gideon's lips. "I think it's best not to be too friendly with my competition."

I snorted. "He's not your competition, Gideon."

He arched his brow. "He would like to be."

I couldn't argue with that. "That may be, but it doesn't matter. I'm only interested in him as a friend."

He watched me with an intense gaze. "Is that how you think of me, too?"

I inhaled a quick breath. "No," I said quietly. "I'm interested in more."

Happiness sparkled in his eyes. "I like the sound of that."

"Besides, I've been thinking I shouldn't be so involved in police investigations. If I backed off, I'd rarely see Corey."

He frowned and shook his head. "But you're passionate about your mysteries."

I shrugged. Was I?

"The Goddess gave you that passion for a reason. You shouldn't ignore it."

I hadn't considered that. "Do you think?"

"Yes. I do. She's set you on this path, and I think you need to follow where it leads."

I wasn't so sure.

I pondered his suggestion for a moment before I took his hand and squeezed it, bringing Nooni's gaze around to see why he'd stopped petting her. "So, speaking of more, I think it's time that I introduce you to my mom. If she hears through the grapevine that we're living together, she won't be happy."

He grinned. "Oh? Your mother? I would love to meet her."

That didn't surprise me in the least. For being a demon, Gideon had the charisma of an angel. "I'm sure you'll have no problem charming the socks off her like you do with everyone."

He winked at me. "I haven't charmed your socks off just yet."

Caught off guard by his insinuation, I dropped my jaw and laughed. Before I could reply, Nicole walked in. Nooni jumped from Gideon's arms and dashed toward her.

Nicole looked at us both and grinned. "Pardon the intrusion, but we have a woman here who'd like to meet Nooni."

EIGHT

I raised my brows at Nicole. "Nooni? We barely got her this morning. Did the shelter send the woman here?"

Nicole's eyes widened with uncertainty. "I don't think so. I believe she's a witch."

My insides tingled. I'd helped over a hundred kitties find their forever homes, which meant a great deal to me. But few of those adoptions had been uniting familiars with their witches. Those experiences were always special.

My friends and I had noticed that Nooni was unique, but I never expected her to have a witch come calling so soon. "Someone we know?"

Nicole shook her head. "I've never seen her before."

I glanced at Gideon and then back to her. I lowered my voice though there wasn't anyone in the room that could hear besides the three of us. "You think she's come to collect her familiar?"

Nicole shrugged. "It's possible this woman sensed that Nooni was here. It happens with some cats who were born already connected to their person."

I couldn't deny the probability. I'd sensed Freya long before I'd met her. When she was old enough to be away from her mother, I received a knowing that I couldn't deny, and it didn't take me long to find her. "Umm...gosh, okay. We barely got her, but if she has a forever home waiting, that's the optimum outcome, right?"

Nicole nodded. "I'll send her in."

When the door closed behind Nicole, Gideon and I stood. He placed his hands on my upper arms and stared into my eyes. "I'm sorry. I'd thought we'd have a little more time to talk this morning, and I wanted to tell you that Nooni had warned me that someone was coming."

Gideon never failed to surprise me. "Are you serious? How is it that you can communicate better with cats than me?"

He gave me a small smile. "I've practiced more."

I frowned. Could it really be that easy?

His expression turned to one of concern. "I don't want you to be sad, okay? This will be best for Nooni."

I studied his face for a moment, not understanding why he'd said that, and then realized he referred to the sadness I'd experienced when my sweet little Angel kitty had recently been adopted. "I'll be fine. Yes, I do get attached to my foster babies, but I haven't had a chance with Nooni. If her person is here, then I'm glad."

The door opened, and he released me. I turned to find a woman in her early thirties, looking smart in a black skirt and silky pink shirt striding in. Her long hair, the color of straw, had been pulled back into a ponytail, and the brown-rimmed glasses she wore accentuated her dark eyes.

She glanced at me with a friendly smile, but when her gaze slid to Gideon, her eyes darkened and the curve of her pink-glossed lips turned sultry.

I knew in an instant that I didn't like her.

She strode forward and addressed me first by holding out her hand. "Hello. I'm Vivian. You must be Daisy."

I reluctantly shook her hand. I'd hoped to encounter a hint of something negative which would give me a reason to turn her away, but she came across as warm and intelligent. "Yes."

She studied me for an awkward moment as though expecting something from me, and then turned to Gideon. She extended her hand again, but this time instead of positioning it for a shake, she held the back of her hand upward. "Hello," she purred.

I blinked in surprise at her overt confidence and prayed that Gideon wouldn't kiss it, like he'd been known to do occasionally.

Instead, he took her hand, twisted it into a quick shake, and released her. "Nice to meet you."

A flirtatious smile teased the corner of her mouth. "I'm sorry. I didn't catch your name."

He gave her a small bow. "Pardon me. Gideon McKay at your service."

I watched as her eyes devoured him from head to toe and back again, and I suspected that she'd completely forgotten I was in the room.

"Gideon. That's a strong name. I sense magic in you, but you're not a witch, correct?"

I cleared my throat before he could answer. "Nicole said that you're here to meet Nooni."

Vivian blinked and shifted her gaze to me. Her smile remained, but I had the distinct impression that she was analyzing me. Then again, I supposed I was doing the same to her.

She glanced down to where the sweet Siamese was rubbing against her legs and knelt. "Yes, I'm here for my companion. Hello, sweetheart."

Nooni's purrs rumbled loudly in the room, and Vivian stroked her head. "Ah, look at you, beautiful lady. You're perfect."

Freya stepped closer to investigate, and Vivian held her fingers out to my cat. She sniffed and then looked up at me, letting me know that she gave her stamp of approval. This led me to wonder if this was something Freya had done all along with other adoptions, and I hadn't noticed.

Vivian drew her hand along Freya's back. "She's yours."

It wasn't a question but a statement, and I wondered again at Vivian's level of intelligence. "Yes, she is. We've been together for more than thirty years."

Vivian scooped up Nooni and stood. She gazed into the cat's eyes, and a euphoric smile curved her lips. "You're lucky then. I've waited a long time for this one, for most things in my life. But my time is now, and good things are coming to me."

She slid her gaze to Gideon, and I swallowed a healthy dose of jealousy. I glanced at him and found him watching me. A hint of a smile played at the corner of his mouth.

Was he enjoying her flirtations?

I sure wasn't.

I returned my gaze to Vivian. I ached to find a reason to deny her, to ask how she could be so certain that Nooni was right for her, but the powerful energy they created together filled the room. "Even though it's destined for you two to be together, I'll still need you to fill out paperwork that the shelter requires and pay the adoption fee. The proceeds go to help care for our fosters and for other animals in need of medical care."

She nodded. "Not a problem." Then she turned to Gideon. "Would you mind holding her?"

Gideon smiled at Nooni. "Of course not."

Knowing that she could have placed the cat on the floor caused me to snort silently.

Vivian made a show of transferring her kitty to Gideon, and I noticed that she didn't miss the opportunity to brush the back of her hand across his chest as she pulled away. Then she reached into the large black leather bag that she carried and withdrew her wallet. She removed a credit card and held it out to me.

I accepted it with a false smile.

A knowing sparked in her eyes, informing me that I hadn't fooled her. On the flip side, she also had to know that Gideon and I were in a relationship.

"Could you get the paperwork for me?" Vivian asked.

"Oh, of course," I said, feeling flustered by her attraction to Gideon. I loathed the emotions her flirtations churned, the memories of similar situations growing up, and the way it stole my concentration.

I walked to the back row of cabinets where we kept supplies and slid open a drawer. The required form was only one page and wouldn't take her long to complete. The sooner she did and left my café, the better.

I returned and held it out. "Here you go. I'll go run your card. If you have questions, I'll be right back."

She gave me a sugary smile. "Take your time. We'll be fine."

I glanced at Gideon, and he gave me a level look. I was certain he must have sensed the energies at play in the room, but other than that bit of a smile that he'd teased me with earlier, he gave no outward hint that he was aware. I swiveled and strode out.

Aeri stood behind the counter and Nicole in front when I emerged. Both watched me with interested gazes. Nicole waited until I was behind the counter before she spoke. "Do they match well?"

I jerked my gaze upward. "No. Of course not."

Nicole frowned. "She seemed certain that Nooni was her cat."

I scoffed. "Oh. Yes. Nooni is her familiar."

Aeri gave me a skeptical look. "Who did you think Nicole was talking about?"

I rolled my eyes. "Vivian. She's flirting with Gideon like she knows he's also her match."

Aeri put a hand on her hip and gave me an incredulous look. "Really?"

Nicole frowned. "The nerve."

I entered the amount of the adoption into the computer, ignored the temptation to add a few extra zeroes to it, and swiped her card. "Oh, she has nerve, all right."

The credit card machine spewed out two copies of the receipt, and I tore them off. I met my friend's gazes with an annoyed look. "I don't want to leave her alone too long."

Nicole shook her head in a reassuring way. "She's not going to steal Gideon from you. In case you haven't noticed, he's completely smitten."

I blinked. "Yes, well, I don't want to find out if smitten can be undone by a younger, prettier, and smarter witch, okay?"

Neither of them argued with me, and I strode back to the Purry Parlor. Inside, I found Gideon still holding Nooni while Vivian stood less than a hand's width away petting her new baby, who seemed content to purr and purr.

When I was near enough, I shoved her credit card and the receipts toward her. "Sign one. The other is yours."

She dropped her hand from Nooni and regarded me as though she didn't understand my irritation. She took what I offered and turned to a nearby counter to sign the receipt. Then she thrust it toward me in the same manner I'd used with her. "Here you go. I left the form on the back counter."

Gideon cleared his throat. "I'll get her loaded into a carrier for you."

I stared at Vivian, trying my best to get a sense of her power, while she watched every move Gideon made. If my eyes had been laser beams, there would be holes in the side of her head. "How far did you have to drive to get here?"

She turned back to me and curved her shiny pink lips into a grin. "Oh, not far at all. I moved to Sweet Mountain Meadows ten days ago. In fact, I don't know if you've sensed it, but we descend from the same line."

I widened my eyes in astonishment. "Of course, I sensed it." Which was a huge lie, but I was admitting to nothing.

She glanced over me, still assessing. "If I would have known that there was a vacant spot on the coven's council, I would have come sooner."

Witch, I wanted to hiss.

That smile on her face was nothing more than a façade.

Gideon stepped forward holding a cardboard carrier with little Nooni inside. Tiny flashes of black around the edges of his irises sparked. If he'd concealed his emotions before, he wasn't now. "Here you go. Be sure that you take good care of her."

His voice was flat and polite and held none of the charm it usually did.

Her gaze turned suspicious but then she smiled. She held out a business card that I hadn't realized she'd had in her hand. "Of course, I'll take care of my precious baby."

Gideon had no choice but to take the card so that she could accept the cat carrier. After the transfer, he glanced down at it and then met her gaze again.

The smile she gave him was slow and sultry. "You should call me. Soon."

With that, Vivian turned and strode toward the door.

"Highly unlikely," Gideon said before she exited the room.

If Vivian heard him, she didn't acknowledge it.

Even after she was gone, the scent of her perfume lingered in the air, and the annoyance she'd stoked in me still thickened my blood. I inhaled a calming breath and released it. "If I wasn't absolutely positive that they belonged together and that she'd take great care of Nooni, I wouldn't have let her walk out the door with her."

He gripped my hand and tugged me toward him until I collided with his chest. He slowly curved his lips into a sexy smile. "If my perceptions were correct, and they usually are, you, my lovely Daisy, were bitten by the jealousy bug."

I scoffed. "No. I just don't like her. Her smug attitude. Her inflated confidence."

He chuckled, and I widened my eyes. "Did *you* like her?"

He kept his beautiful blue eyes trained on me. "She was of little consequence to me. I didn't like or dislike her."

I huffed my frustration, wishing I could have felt the same. "Well, she certainly liked you."

He drew the tips of his fingers down my cheek. "You are the only one who holds my affections, Daisy."

I held his gaze as his words sank into my heart. Then he kissed me.

Slow, sweet, soft. Then the kiss quickly became heated.

"Daisy—whoa. Sorry!" Nicole said and retreated from the room, but her intrusion had been enough to break the spell he'd cast over me.

I put my fingertips to my mouth and chuckled. "It's a good thing that you're meeting my mom soon because I don't think I can keep you hidden much longer."

He lifted interested brows. "I like the sound of that."

I laughed, thinking how his kiss had significantly improved my mood. "I'd better see what Nicole needs."

NINE

An hour before closing the next day, I left Aeri and Nicole in charge of Meowkins. Gideon had taken the kitties and gone home several hours before, needing to change before he headed out for a "meeting".

I feared that I knew what kind of meeting he meant, a person wanting to exchange their soul for love or money, but I didn't ask. Or, I suppose, he could have been going to collect a soul whose time had expired. To me, it seemed wrong that someone could have the power to do that, but I had to accept that the Goddess knew more than I did. She strived for a balance of power and energy, which I knew was important.

For now, I had other things to worry about, mainly the fact that I was headed out to visit my mom. I felt that telling her that I had a new man in my life, let alone that we were living together, seemed to merit an in-person visit instead of a phone call. Afterward, I planned to meet Nicole at The Expanding Universe for a nice, relaxing yoga class.

It was a sunny, but blustery day. Clouds had rolled in like the meteorologist had predicted, though we wouldn't likely receive any moisture. Tree limbs waved in the breeze, and more than once, debris skittered across the road in front of me.

Not far into my drive, I spotted Bobbi Knowles sitting on a bus bench outside the grocery store holding several shopping bags. She obviously needed a ride, and my conscience wouldn't let me drive past without stopping. I wanted to see how she and her daughter were doing now that a few days had passed since Karyn's murder, and if Bobbi would let me, I'd give her a ride home.

I pulled past the bus stop and parked my car. Bobbi was focused on her phone and didn't see me until I was close.

She seemed surprised to see me, but she didn't shy away or give me a look of warning, so I assumed it was okay to approach. "Hey, Bobbi. I was just driving past and saw you. Can I give you a lift somewhere?"

A look of relief washed over her face. "You wouldn't mind?"

I snorted. "Of course not. I'm headed to my mom's for a quick visit, but I have time before I need to be there. Let me help you with those."

I sensed her gratitude as she passed three grocery bags full of food to me, keeping the other four and a gallon of milk for herself, and then she stood.

Her smile didn't diminish the dark shadows hovering beneath her eyes, though. She glanced at me as we walked to my car. "Normally, I would go with Karyn to the store, and she'd drive. Today, Alisha needed to take my car to Salt Lake. I would have waited until the weather was better tomorrow to do the shopping, but we're all out of milk."

"Well, it seems like the universe was looking out for you and sent me your way."

We piled the groceries into the trunk and settled into my car. "You'll need to give me directions since I don't know where you live."

She pushed her long hair back from her face. "I live in the guest house behind Karyn's. When she hired me, she asked if I would mind living on site so that I could be available if she needed me. Plus, making breakfast for her and Sailor each day was part of my duties, so it made sense to be close, and it also saved me on rent."

I nodded in understanding. "That seems nice."

She smiled, and then her expression crumbled into tears. "It was nice. At some point soon, Alisha and I will have to look for a new place to live."

I knew that worry far too well. "I get that. I recently lost my lease and had to find a new place, too. Packing everything and then settling somewhere else isn't much fun."

She sniffed. "I keep hoping that Sailor will want to keep living in her mom's house and that we can stay, but I bet she'll want to move in with her dad. She's extremely responsible, but she's not quite an adult yet. Plus, Karyn's house is a big place, and too much room for a person so young."

I hadn't connected that Karyn's death would also mean additional losses for Bobbi. "I'm so sorry. I didn't realize that you might lose your housing along with your housekeeping job, on top of losing your friend."

The weight of her situation hung heavy in her expression. "Yeah."

I drew my brows in concern. "I hear that the studio will continue to operate. Will you keep your job there?"

She wiped her tears. "For now. It's all I have. But I'll have to look for something full-time so that I can pay rent."

My heart broke for the poor woman. "Joel Adams might be able to help you find a reasonable, good place to live, and I'll let you know if I hear of anyone looking to hire, okay?"

She hugged her purse tight against her stomach. "Thank you. I truly appreciate that."

Liza's comments about Bobbi also having issues with Karyn kept creeping into my thoughts, so I acknowledged them. "I spoke with Liza not long ago."

Bobbi lifted her gaze to me. "Oh, yeah? What did she say?"

"I asked her if she'd been arguing with Karyn, and she admitted to it."

Bobbi nodded. "She'd better. Too many people saw her, and she'd be caught in a lie if she said otherwise."

I lifted a cautious brow as I turned onto the street where Karyn had lived. "She said you'd also been having problems with her."

A pained expression twisted Bobbi's features, and she nodded. "Karyn hadn't been herself lately, and she could sometimes be a hard person to please."

Silence filled the space between us as I considered my next words.

Bobbi shifted in the seat to face me and spoke softly. "I didn't hurt Karyn, if that's what you're wondering. Even though she could be a big pain and very demanding sometimes, I liked her. I liked working for her. She was good to me that way. Our girls are best friends, and Karyn was always generous with me. Working for her and living there allowed Alisha to go to much better schools, too."

I pulled to the back of the driveway, nearest to the small guest house, and parked. I met her gaze. "No, I'm not accusing you."

She gave me a quick nod. "Thank you. I know it sounds awful to say, but I had a lot of reasons besides friendship to still want her to be alive. This has completely upended Alisha's and my lives. She hurts for Sailor's loss, and Karyn was like a second mother to her."

I reached over and squeezed her hand. "I'll do what I can to help. If you need anything, please let me know, okay?"

She gave me a grateful smile. "Thank you so much."

A few minutes later, I was back in my car and headed to my mom's. I tried hard to put Bobbi's devastation out of my mind, but it seemed determined to creep back in. There had to be a way to help her. Maybe my friends and I could come up with something.

TEN

I knocked lightly on my mom's front door to give her a heads-up that I was coming in and then turned the knob. Once inside, I checked the sitting room where she loved to spend her days looking out the picturesque window at the mountains towering above her and reading. Though recently, on more than one occasion, I'd come over and found her crocheting the edges of flannel baby blankets. They were for people in town, she'd said, and I hoped she meant it because babies were not on the horizon for me.

This afternoon, though, her sitting room was empty.

I peeked into the kitchen before I searched upstairs for her and came up empty-handed. Fear crept into my thoughts. Knowing that Gideon had inadvertently made me a possible target for a rogue demon led me to worry that it could extend to my mother as well.

I scrambled down the stairs in a hurry, calling her name as I went. "Mum? Where are you?"

I heard a muffled voice coming from the kitchen and hurried in that direction. When I burst in, I found her on her knees in front of an open oven. Yellow rubber gloves covered her hands, and she sang as she scrubbed. "Mum," I said in a rush of relief.

She continued singing and scrubbing, not paying me any notice. When I moved closer, I noticed the earbuds peeking from beneath the short gray hair near her ears and scoffed in disbelief. I didn't even know my mom knew what earbuds were, let alone how to use them with her phone.

"Mum," I said louder and tapped her on the shoulder.

She yelped and whirled her head around, brandishing her sponge as a weapon. When she saw that it was only me, she shook her head in annoyance and pulled the buds from her ears. "Daisy Mae. What are you trying to do? Give me a heart attack?"

I opened my hands wide in defense. "I called out, but you were too into your music. How loud do you have the volume?"

She waved away my concern and tucked the buds into her pocket. Then she thrust a hand out toward me. "Here, help me up."

Once she was on her feet, it took her a moment to fully straighten, and she groaned as she did.

I shut the oven door and turned to her with disapproval. "Why are you cleaning your oven?"

"Because it was dirty."

"Mum," I said with a fair amount of admonishment. "It hasn't been that long since you've had surgery. You should be taking it easy."

She pushed past me and headed for the small wooden table for two that she'd purchased a year ago and sat. I followed her over, unwilling to let her off the hook. "How exactly did you expect to get off the floor if I hadn't stopped by?"

Her gaze grew stern. "I'm capable of managing myself. If I sit around doing nothing much longer, then I'll be forced to do that the rest of my life. Mona says I gotta keep moving."

I snorted, thinking of the older witch with bright red hair. She always had a smile on her face, but she lacked some in the brains department. "And Mona is an expert now, is she?"

My mom's expression grew snarky. "I'd say she's aged rather well for an eighty-year-old, wouldn't you?"

Mona's age was news to me. "She's that old? I never would have guessed."

But I could hardly argue her fitness knowledge after witnessing her stamina at the workout studio.

My mom shrugged as if to say that Mona and she were smarter than I gave them credit for. "Will you get me a glass of water, please?"

I wanted to retort that if she was so spry, she should do it herself. But regardless of her admirable can-do attitude, my mom was pushing it if she thought she could do everything.

I filled two glasses with ice and water and sat with her at the table.

She took a large drink and sighed as she set the glass down. "I'm surprised to see you here today. You didn't mention that you'd stop by."

"I'm actually on my way to the Expanding Universe. I told Nicole I'd take a yoga class with her."

My mom nodded in approval. "That's right. Mona said she saw you there the night Karyn died. I'm sure the classes will do you some good."

I frowned. "What does that mean? Are you saying I'm out of shape?"

Karyn had proven that to be true the other day, but my mom didn't know it. Ugh. Unless Mona had tattled on me.

She shrugged. "It's like I said. Gotta use it or lose it."

I was starting to believe there might be some truth to the fact that one should listen to her elders.

My mom took another drink. "I'm surprised the studio is back open so quickly."

I shrugged. "Me, too. But I guess life doesn't stop for the rest of us. People need their jobs, and clients want to work out."

Interest sparkled in her eyes. "What's the latest on the investigation? Have you learned anything new?"

"Why does everyone keep asking me that? Corey...the police are capable of doing their job."

She clucked at me like she'd always done in my youth when she thought I was lying. "You know that you like to be in the middle of things like that. Isn't that part of your coven duties anyway?"

"To solve murders? I'm pretty sure it's not."

She didn't seem convinced. "Peace and prosperity."

I snorted. "Karyn isn't even part of the coven."

She widened her eyes in innocence. "Well, a murder does affect the mood of the whole town, doesn't it? We'd all like to feel safe, knowing the person who did it was behind bars."

This conversation had fallen down a rabbit hole. Time was running out before I needed to leave and meet Nicole, but I seemed incapable of blurting out anything about Gideon.

I took a drink of water, reminding myself that it wasn't a bad idea to hydrate before working out. I needed to stop distracting myself from the real reason I was there, but I couldn't help it.

Another thought popped into my head, and I focused on my mom. "Let me ask you a question since you think I should be doing more for the coven. Why are you unwilling to show me everything in your magical chest? I'm fully participating with the council now, and you might have something that could help me."

My reasoning was a stretch, but seriously, what was she hiding?

She winked at me. "All in good time."

I frowned. "What's that supposed to mean?"

Her expression remained calm. "Jocelyn asked me to go slow."

That didn't sit right with me. "Jocelyn? Why is she in the middle of things that concern our family?"

My mom gifted me with a matter-of-fact look. "She's the wisest in our coven. I didn't ask for her reasons, but I trust her."

"Instead of trusting me?"

She chuckled and patted the back of my hand. "Don't worry. You'll get what you need when you need it."

I huffed in disgust.

She exhaled a large sigh and put a hand on the table between us. "I'm certain you didn't stop by to argue. Let's talk about something else. How goes the house search? You'd mentioned you might be looking to buy something. Any luck?"

Her words had segued right where I needed them to, but I still struggled to disclose my secret. Then the thought of someone else telling my mom about Gideon forced my hand. "Truth be told, that's part of the reason I stopped by. I wanted to let you know that I'm going to be staying in the cottage for a while."

She smiled. "It's such a darling place. Is your friend going to be away for longer?"

I swallowed, trying to ease the tightness in my throat. "Actually, he's back in town now."

She frowned. "Doesn't he want to live there?"

I released a stress-filled sigh and smiled. "We're roommates."

She lifted her brows in surprise. "*Roommates?* With a man? Are you lovers, then?"

Trust my mom to jump right to the heart of the matter. "No." Though I expected that might not remain the truth for long.

"I thought you said you didn't know him well. And now you're living with him?"

She did have a point. "It's complicated, Mum."

Her eyes narrowed in suspicion. "From my experience, complicated usually means trouble. Is he married?"

I scoffed. "No, of course not. I have enough respect not to put myself in that situation."

"Well, that's good, at least."

I gave her a gentle smile. "What I'd like to do is introduce you to him so that you can see what he's like for yourself. We could have you over for dinner. He's a great cook."

That seemed to mollify her a little. "Well, maybe. What's he like?"

I felt the smile blossoming on my face but couldn't temper it. "Gideon's great. Kind and considerate. A true gentleman. He loves cats and coffee, so we have that in common."

She studied me for a moment and then smiled. "My goodness. You love him."

I opened my mouth to reject her idea, but she held up a hand. "Don't try to convince me otherwise. If I meet him, I'll know anyway."

What could I say to that? She would indeed be able to read me. "So, that's a yes, you'll come? This Sunday, maybe?"

She nodded, and relief gushed through me. "What does this Gideon do for a living? And why did he decide to move to Sweet Mountain?"

I drew my tongue across my bottom lip to moisten it. "His job doesn't require him to live anywhere in particular. He was in town during Beltane and decided he liked it enough to buy a place here."

I didn't add that he'd purchased the cottage to help me.

My mom seemed agreeable to the situation, allowing me to relax a little. "That's nice," she said. "It's hard not to fall in love with our little town. You didn't say what his job is, though."

My thoughts choked and sputtered, and I spewed the first thing that came into my head. "Commodities. He deals in commodities."

Her smile widened. "Oh, that's nice. Commodities can be lucrative, and it sounds like he's done well with them."

I nodded. "Yeah. I know his boss is pleased with his work."

My throat tightened again after the lie. I slugged down the rest of my water and stood. "I should get going if I'm going to make it to the studio before class starts. I'll come pick you up around five on Sunday. Does that sound okay?"

She beamed with a happy smile and nodded. "That sounds wonderful. I'm looking forward to meeting your man."

A blush heated my face, and I leaned close to kiss her cheek before she noticed. "Love you," I called as I turned away. "See you soon."

I cursed myself for the untruth as I strode out her door. But it couldn't be helped at this point. Gideon needed a chance to charm her like he'd done with me before I let her know that her daughter had fallen in love with a demon.

ELEVEN

The scent of sweet lemongrass tickled my senses as I entered the Expanding Universe, reminding me of the last time I'd been in the building and Karyn's punishing workout. At the time, neither of us had known it would be her last class.

But this time, instead of high energy vibrating in the atmosphere, a somber mood hovered in the air. I knew that whoever was in charge, likely Karyn's ex-husband, was keeping the studio going, probably because clients had paid for services that they had yet to receive. Or perhaps Karyn's daughter, Sailor, wanted it to remain open in her mother's memory.

Either way, they needed to smudge to clear the negative energy from the space, or people would automatically stop attending. Most people who exercised craved that energetic high, and that would be harder to find if the place stayed the way it was.

Earlier, I hadn't paid much attention to the large photo on the wall behind the reception desk of a man and woman, but I stepped closer to inspect it this time. Karyn was obviously the woman in the picture. A small placard at the bottom of the frame told me that her ex-husband, Ian Strickland was the other person. The framed picture had been placed to commemorate the opening of the Expanding Universe.

I studied Ian's face in the photo, his dark hair and cool expression, the way his height allowed him to tower over Karyn. "Did you do it?" I whispered. "Because we'll find out if you did."

The sound of a woman laughing caught my attention, and I turned my back on the photo. Instead of heading into the main studio where I'd worked out before, I followed signs and walked down the now-lit hall where I'd caught Liza kissing Justin. I didn't know if Liza was guilty or not, but I didn't envy her being spotlighted as a main suspect.

I strolled into the room where ten or so people sat on rolled out yoga mats in various colors, and Mona with her bright red hair caught my attention and grinned. "Good to see you," she called in a loud voice. Instead of yelling back, I smiled and nodded.

Nicole caught my attention with a wave, and I headed in her direction. I intended to tell her about Bobbi's unfortunate situation and see if she had ideas to help her.

That was until I heard someone call my name and turned to find the witch Vivian looking smart and toned in her all-black workout gear. I hadn't recognized her with her back to me and her hair up, but once our gazes connected, my emotions hardened. I forced a smile, and she gave me a wave that would have seemed friendly coming from anyone else.

She could act innocent as much as she liked, but I knew her true motives. She wanted Gideon, and I was in the way.

For a moment, I wondered if that's how Gideon felt about Corey. Perhaps, I should have been more sensitive to his feelings, and I vowed to be so in the future.

I turned my back to Vivian, made a face, and continued toward Nicole.

She had a bright pink mat waiting for me next to her purple one. I set my bag along the wall near her and sank to the mat with a sideways glance in her direction. "Vivian's here."

She gave me a snarky look. "Yeah, I noticed."

I sighed and pushed away the negative energy that Vivian's appearance had created. I inhaled, closed my eyes, and connected with the warm source inside me. Then I blew out a cleansing breath. "I'm just going to pretend that she doesn't exist."

Liza walked in wearing a periwinkle sports bra and black leggings, with hair pulled back into a ponytail. She smiled at a few people in the front, though I could see the heaviness of the past few days weighing on her features. "Good evening, everyone. I hope you've come with an open mind and an open heart. Let's get started on releasing the tension from your day."

That sounded perfect to me.

Liza glanced around the room, her eyes briefly narrowing when she spotted me. "Let's start in a cross-legged position. Sukhasana. The pose of ease. Loop your shoulders a few times, up and back."

I watched Nicole and emulated her actions, immediately feeling the stretch of tight muscles at the base of my neck.

"Check in with your breath," Liza continued.

I glanced about the room to see what others were doing with their breath. Most had their eyes closed as they rolled their shoulders, but that's as much as I could see. I decided that as long as I was breathing, everything was good. I lowered my lids and focused on loosening my muscles.

Liza released a deep exhale. "Coming back to center, let's bring the head over the heart, the heart over the pelvis."

I opened my eyes to watch Liza's movements and found her staring at me with a dark expression. She quickly looked away.

I turned my head toward Nicole to whisper. "She doesn't like us here."

Nicole gave a small shake of her head. "Nope," she said quietly. "Can't imagine why."

"Exactly."

I did my best to block Liza's energy as well, turning my focus inward to my body and breaths. I did a pretty good job keeping up with the class until I lost my balance during the warrior one pose and tumbled to the floor. Someone snickered, and Nicole glanced over her shoulder. I didn't need to look to know it was Vivian.

It wasn't until the heart-to-earth pose, when we all had our butts in the air, that someone upstaged me. The sound of passing gas ripped through the room, followed by Mona's giggle. I did my best not to laugh and decided if she wasn't embarrassed over that, I wouldn't be for the tumble.

An hour later, we'd finished my favorite part, savasana, and I was sad that the class was over. Though my body felt like I'd been strung out on a medieval stretching rack, my mind was clear, and delicious energy flowed freely through me.

I glanced at Nicole.

She must have sensed my emotions because she gave me one of her signature big smiles. "Better?" she asked.

I nodded. "This beat the other class hands-down."

Happiness brightened her expression. "So, you'll want to come again?"

I exhaled and smiled. "Sure. I think I'd like it. Though from the looks Liza kept shooting in my direction, I'm not so sure she'll approve."

Nicole gave me a nonchalant shrug. "That's her problem."

I pointed to the pink mat I'd used. "Where do I put this?"

She chuckled. "Oh, it's yours. I bought it for you."

I shouldn't have been surprised. "I could have hated yoga for all you knew."

"Nah, I knew you wouldn't."

I lifted a questioning brow.

She smiled and linked her arm through mine. "Oh, Daisy. You like to pretend that no one knows the real you, but I think Aeri and I have a pretty good sense of what goes on in your head. Whether you like it or not."

Truth was, I sort of liked it and hated it at the same time. It was nice that my friends knew me, until they used insider information against me. For my own good, they'd always say.

Though I supposed I did the same to them. "Well, thanks. That was nice of you."

She gave me a mischievous grin. "Anything for my new workout partner. Why don't you roll your mat while I grab our bags?"

I basked in the flood of oxygen that saturated my veins and grabbed the edge of my mat. I'd barely begun to roll it when I sensed someone nearby and looked up. Vivian towered over me with a crafty twinkle in her eyes. "You think he's yours."

Her comment caught me off guard, and I blinked. "Excuse me?"

She chuckled. "You think he's yours, but we both know who he really belongs to."

Unable to form a response, I dropped my jaw, and she turned away. I stared as she left the room, and then startled when Nicole rejoined me. "You okay?" she asked.

I shook my head to settle my thoughts. "Vivian just told me that I think Gideon is mine when she and I both know who he really belongs to."

She dropped down next to me with a stunned look. "What? She really said that to you?"

I nodded matter-of-factly. "I told you she was after him."

"But he's not interested in her at all. You know that."

The disturbing incident replayed in my head. "Apparently, she believes that doesn't matter. Or she thinks she can change his mind."

Neither of which was remotely okay with me.

With a wave of her hand and a few whispered words, Nicole whisked away the negative energy Vivian had left behind. "Forget her. She's obviously a few marbles short. If she tries anything, I'll hex her."

I snorted. It was a nice thing for Nicole to say, but I had no doubt that Vivian's intelligence ranked up there with the best of witches. "I'm not going to let you risk Karma's wrath for her."

She grinned. "Maybe not, but Aeri and I've still got your back. Let her try taking us on."

I laughed though irritation still lingered inside me. "Hey, I did get my mom to agree to come to dinner on Sunday to meet Gideon."

Nicole lifted her brows in interest. "That's great. Have you already told her that you're living together?"

"I had to after she asked where my friend was staying while I was in his house."

"Oh...how did that go over?"

I shrugged. "She had a lot of questions, but in the end, she seemed okay with it."

Nicole lifted her bag and slid it onto her shoulder. "What about the other thing?" she asked quietly.

I sighed and shook my head. "Yeah, I'm not sure when I'll mention that. Luckily, only a few of us in town know about Gideon's occupation, so that gives me time. I'm hoping she'll fall in love with his charm and kind heart enough so that when I do tell her, she'll be able to see that he's much more than his job."

We headed for the door, and she reassured me with a smile. "I don't think you need to worry about that. It's hard not to love him after even one conversation. He's like the best guy."

As we neared the exit, Liza strode toward us with an unhappy look on her face. She focused on me. "What are you doing here? Why can't you stay out of my life?"

The surprise attack rattled me. "What?"

Her gaze darkened into something completely opposite of the soothing music that played. "You've never come to this class before. Why now, huh? Don't think I don't know what you're doing."

I shot a quick glance at Nicole and found her expression just as shocked. "I'm not sure what you're thinking, but I came tonight because Nicole invited me. She thought I might like it better than the one we did with Karyn the other night."

She smirked. "Uh-huh. Right. I know you're spying on me. Watching to see if I'll do something."

I really didn't want to have this conversation with her. In fact, I wasn't sure if I wanted to involve myself in this case more than I already had, but I didn't appreciate her accusations, either. "You're acting awfully defensive, Liza, which hints more at guilt than innocence."

Nicole nodded. "You might want to check your attitude."

Liza's cheeks colored. "Don't lie to me. Everyone in town knows that Daisy likes to insert herself into investigations."

I drew my brows in surprise. "They do?"

Liza narrowed her gaze in response.

I shook my head and snorted. "Honestly, I was here for the class, but since you're insistent on pushing things, I'll let you know that I spoke to Bobbi."

She pointed an accusing finger at me. "See? You can't stay out of it."

I rolled my eyes. "I gave her a ride home, okay? She brought it up. She did admit that she had difficulty with Karyn sometimes, but I can't see that Karyn's death benefitted her in any way. In fact, it hurt her. Her job duties have diminished, and now she'll have to find a new place to live."

Liza opened her mouth, then closed it, and then chose to speak anyway. "Maybe she should have done that from the start instead of siphoning off Karyn's goodwill."

I gasped. "Ouch, Liza. That's pretty harsh."

She shrugged. "I'm just calling it like it is. Did you know Bobbi is in her will?"

That froze me in my tracks. "No, I didn't." And my mind followed the trail Liza had led me to. "Are you in it as well?"

She scoffed. "As if. One, I don't need her money any more than I apparently needed her friendship. And two, I wouldn't want it anyway. It's sad that it took her death to make me realize what a negative force she was in my life."

I glanced at Nicole, who was looking as uncomfortable as I felt. "We should go."

"Yup," Nicole responded.

Liza gripped my arm. "Before you get too focused on me, try looking at her ex-husband, too. He still owns half this studio and tried to get Karyn to sell it about three months ago, but she wouldn't relinquish her last hold on him."

I pulled my arm away. "I'm not looking at anyone, Liza. I already told you that."

"Then Sailor," she called as we made our way to the door.

I turned and looked back at her. "I have nothing to do with this."

Her look had turned to desperation. "Sailor was always asking her mom for money that she'd turn around and waste on a new pair of shoes. Or drugs. Everyone knows she likes to party."

I lifted a hand to stop her. "Tell it to the police."

I hurried through the door and didn't slow down until we'd reached the cooler evening air.

Nicole thumbed over her shoulder toward the building. "What was that all about?"

I shook my head in bewilderment. "I'm not sure. But she's acting awfully guilty."

"That she is. I'm still not certain she and Justin weren't in on it together."

I shot a sideways glance toward my friend. "How well do you know him? Ever had much contact with him here before?"

"No, I've never been in the weight room. That's his Jeep, though. I've seen him driving it."

I followed the direction of her finger toward the front of the parking lot and spotted a bright yellow Jeep. "Everything about him is showy, it seems."

She chuckled. "That's a great description of him. I think one of his favorite things about working at the studio is all the attention he gets from the ladies."

Her insight didn't help much, but at least it was something.

We parted ways, and I headed to my car. As hard as I tried, I couldn't keep scenarios of what might have happened to Karyn from playing repeatedly in my mind. I truly wanted to distance myself from the case, but it seemed the fates had plans for something else, and I wasn't sure how to reconcile that.

Perhaps Gideon with his sound advice might help me.

TWELVE

When I arrived home, the scent of something delicious greeted me, and my stomach cried out with happy rumbles. Unfortunately, Gideon had left the pot simmering on the stove and a note on the table that said he'd been called away unexpectedly. After what Vivian had said to me, I really wanted to fold myself into his embrace, but I supposed I would have to wait.

I'd just finished a long shower, donned comfy jammies, and settled onto the couch with a murder mystery and a glass of wine, when my phone rang. I frowned when I saw my mother's name on the screen. I tried to ward off a sense of doom as I tapped the screen to answer. "Mum? Are you okay?"

"I am fine," she said in a stilted voice. "I... Could you come over for a minute. I need to talk to you."

I sucked in a tense breath, wondering what might be up. "You okay?"

"Yes. I've spoken with Jocelyn, and I need to see you."

My sense of doom immediately shifted to excitement. If she'd spoken to Jocelyn, perhaps the leader of our coven had agreed that it was time for me to receive something else from my mother's chest of secrets. Maybe after my recent success with Herman Huber's ghost, my time had come. "Sure, Mum. I'll be right over."

Freya met me at my front door and glanced up at me expectantly. "Do you want to come with me?"

She meowed in the affirmative, so I picked her up and headed out. I didn't bother to take the time to change since I was only going to my mom's. I also might have exceeded the speed limit a few times as I hurried down the mountain to her house.

I parked, lifted Freya, and held her against my chest. As I exited, I spied Jocelyn's car parked along the street, and my anticipation increased. The high priestess was at my mom's house. That had to mean this was something important.

I tested my mom's doorknob, found it unlocked, and stepped inside.

The scent of magic was heavy in the air, and I breathed deeply. Whatever the two had been doing required powerful energy and intrigued me to the tips of my toes.

I found them in my mother's sitting room, my mom in her chair, and Jocelyn on the nearby couch where I usually sat. I dropped Freya to the floor as I glanced between both of their faces and found solemn expressions. My mind tried to justify the reasons why they'd look that way in relation to me receiving more gifts, but I couldn't make the connection. "Hey, Mum. Hi, Jocelyn."

The high priestess stood, sending the hem of her bright purple skirt rushing to the floor. Her long gray braid hung over one shoulder, and though I searched her expression, I couldn't read any emotion in her dark blue eyes.

She held out a hand toward me, and light from a nearby table lamp glinted off the many silver bangles encircling her wrist. "Come, Daisy. Sit."

Freya's claws sank through my soft pajama shirt and into my skin, warning me. "What's wrong?"

My mother dropped her face into her palm and sniffed, freaking me out more than a little.

Jocelyn motioned me forward. "Come and sit."

I strode closer and took her hand. A frisson of powerful vibes entered through my skin, surrounding me with strength and protective energy. I stared into her wise face, lined with years of learned knowledge and life experiences. "Did someone die?"

I couldn't imagine why they'd be acting that way otherwise. "Mum?" I said, but she wouldn't look at me.

Jocelyn didn't speak until we were both seated on the couch next to each other. "We've recently come across information that puts you in grave danger."

I sucked in a worried breath, wondering how they'd learned of Sauron, the rogue demon who might be after me. "Tell me."

Jocelyn gazed at me with love and wonder. "You have a beautiful soul, Daisy."

I drew my brows together. "Thank you."

She nodded approvingly. "Your mother and I would like to keep it that way."

I glanced toward my mom who now watched from the corner of her eye. "As would I."

Jocelyn squeezed my hand, drawing my attention back to her. "You are aware that Gideon is a demon?"

My pulse spiked to an uncomfortable high, and my throat tightened. "I am. But he's not what you'd expect from such a person."

The wise high priestess waved her other hand between us. "Your thoughts have been compromised, Daisy. You must not trust them."

I frowned and pulled my hand from hers. "I don't believe that's true."

"Of course, you don't," my mom said with a fearful look in her eye. "He has you, and I can't lose you forever."

Great Goddess. This was not happening.

I gasped and stood. "That's simply not true, Mum. Do I seem like a different person? As if someone has taken control of me? No.

Gideon has a kind heart and a good soul. If you would meet him, you'd see that."

Jocelyn stood and took my hand once again. Energy surged through me, and this time, I recognized it. "You've done a cleansing spell on me? And a protection spell? I didn't ask for that."

My mother got to her feet and sent me a wild look. "Don't let him take you, Daisy. I can't lose you."

I extracted my hand once again and took a step back. "Where is this coming from? Who told you about Gideon?"

Jocelyn shook her head. "That doesn't matter."

"Who told you?" I demanded.

The high priestess conceded with a dip of her head. "Vivian Fowler passed along the information, and I confirmed it for myself. I'm certain if I were to go to his house, your house, I would find that it reeks of the darkness."

I dropped my jaw. They'd gone too far, had insulted the man I loved too much. I took another step back. "As wise as you both are, you're completely mistaken in Gideon's case. He's a good man. The work he does is just that, his job."

Jocelyn shook her head. "It can't be both."

Heartbreak welled up inside me. "It can, and it is. And I love him."

My mother broke into tears as my childhood world crumbled around me.

But I wouldn't back down. "I'm sorry that you can't see it. But you're going to have to give him a chance, Mum. There is no other option."

She turned to Jocelyn with a crazed look in her eyes. "Can we sedate her? Give her time to come back to herself?"

Horror rushed through me.

Jocelyn watched me with a calm that infuriated me. "It's not too late to make a better choice, Daisy. It's nearly Midsummer. The perfect time to choose a new path. If you won't for yourself, then do it for your poor mother."

Using my love for my mom against me had the opposite effect of what she'd expected. "Do what you've gotta do, Jocelyn. Kick me off the council. Whatever. But hear this. Even if you did drug me, it would change nothing. I'm the only one who owns my soul."

The high priestess shook her head. "It's the goddess's choice who serves on the council. Not mine."

I snorted. "Well, if she hasn't indicated a different choice, obviously she thinks my decisions are fine."

I'd had enough of their craziness. I sent my mom one last pleading look and then turned from them, hurrying from the house before their intervention turned into a kidnapping.

Tears streamed down my face as I ran toward my car. I tripped on the raised piece of cement that I normally remembered and tumbled toward the ground.

Before I hit, strong hands caught me and righted me. "Gideon," I gasped.

He searched my face. "What's wrong?"

I blinked away tears, glanced at my mother's house, and then focused on him.

In turn, he shifted his gaze toward the house, and his eyes darkened.

"Demon," Jocelyn called from the porch step. "I command you to release her. To release her soul."

He closed his eyes for a brief moment, and I sensed the anguish burning inside him. Then he focused on Jocelyn. "I'm afraid, madame, that you are mistaken. I have no desire to claim Daisy's soul. Her heart, perhaps, but that is all. She has nothing to fear from me. Nor do you."

I expected Jocelyn to lift a hand and send a curse flailing toward us, but she remained still. I shifted my gaze upward to Gideon. "Please, let's go. I need to be away from here."

He cupped my chin with his hand and searched my face. "As you wish. I'll drive."

I shook my head. "No. I can't leave my car here. I'll need it, and I don't want to come back later. Not until they can see reason."

He sighed and brushed tears from my cheeks. "Then I'll follow you home."

Jocelyn stayed on the porch, watching us while he walked me to my car. I climbed inside, sent him a watery smile, and started the engine. I focused on the road ahead of me as I pulled away.

Gideon didn't immediately follow, and I began to worry that Jocelyn might have tried something after I'd left. But then a few moments later, I recognized the sound of his car's powerful engine as he drove up behind me.

Tears threatened to fall again, but I held them back until I'd made it up the mountain for fear that I might hit a deer if I didn't control my emotions. But once I was parked in the driveway, I dropped my head and sobbed in earnest.

I couldn't believe I hadn't seen this one coming. How could I have missed it? When Vivian had said that we both knew who Gideon belonged to, she hadn't meant herself or me.

She thought he belonged to the dark.

But she was wrong.

He also belonged to me.

THIRTEEN

Moments after I'd parked my car, Gideon opened my door and pulled me into his arms. "I'm so sorry, my lovely. You deserve better than this. Better than me."

My throat was too clogged with emotion to speak, so I met his gaze with defiance and shook my head.

He scooped me into his arms and carried me toward the house. I caught sight of Freya dashing toward the door and gasped because I'd completely forgotten her at my mom's. "Freya."

He gave me a gentle smile as he carried me inside and sat me on the couch. "Don't worry. I waited for her as she ran for my car."

I blinked back tears and gave him a grateful smile. "Thank you."

The fact that Freya had willingly run to him cemented the fact in my heart that Gideon was the right man for me.

He tugged my shoes from my feet and wrapped me in a soft forest green quilt. Then he led me to the couch, sat next to me, and pulled me into his embrace. I fell softly against his chest and didn't move as grief washed over and through me. I shivered at the intensity of it.

Gideon snapped his fingers, and a fire roared to life in the fireplace. His ability shouldn't have surprised me. I turned and gazed up at him. "You can light fires?"

He chuckled though his eyes still held traces of the emotional damage that had been done that day. "How do you think the fires of Hell came to be?"

I lifted my brows in disbelief. "You did not do that."

He smiled and slowly shook his head. "Not me, my lovely. Another demon, but by the same method, with the same kind of magic."

I nodded in understanding and rested my head against his chest again.

He drew the side of his thumb down my cheek. "I'll not ask you to talk about it now, but I'm here when you're ready."

I snuggled harder against his chest, finding comfort in the sound of his beating heart.

Several moments of silence passed before he spoke again. "If, as you process this, you discover that your place is not with me, I'll understand."

I whirled my head to face him. "No. That will never happen."

I shook my head vehemently to drive my point home.

He gave me a kind smile. "But if it does...okay?"

"No. Never. Life has led me down a very different road than the one I'd been on, and I have no idea what will happen next, but I want you with me. I need you with me."

I wasn't certain I'd convinced him, but he didn't argue again.

I stared at him for a long while and then laid my head on his chest and closed my eyes. I could feel his love anchored deep in my heart, and I knew if I or someone else tried to rip it out, it would destroy me.

At some point, I must have drifted off, because the next thing I knew I was in his arms again as he carried me down the hall toward my bedroom. Inside, he carefully placed me on the bed and tried to settle the quilt around me. I caught his hand and held it. "Don't leave me, Gideon."

He gave me a smile full of love. "Never fear, Daisy. If we are to be separated, it will be you that will have to leave me."

He tried to pull his hand from mine, but I held tighter. "I mean now. Don't leave me now. Stay. Here with me."

His brows shot upward in surprise and drew a smile from deep in my heart. "Are you saying..."

I sighed, unable to contain the burning need to connect with him. "Yes, that's exactly what I'm saying. I want you with me, here, now, and always. Stay with me, Gideon, and let me love you."

The quiet disbelief that played across his handsome face burrowed deep into my heart.

He pulled the loose cotton shirt that he wore over his head and dropped it to the floor. I scooted over to make room for him, and once he was settled next to me, I kissed him until any doubt he might have had about my true feelings disappeared into the haze of love.

****

When I woke the next morning, Gideon was gone, leaving only a red rose on the pillow where he'd slept. My heart still ached after what had happened with my mom and Jocelyn, but there was a part of me that felt full and whole and happy. My mom had been right when she'd said that love would find me someday. I only wished I could share that with her now.

But the time would come. I would find a way to bring them together so that she would be able to look past the label of demon and could meet the man who'd stolen my heart.

With that intention lit and burning inside me, I rose and found breakfast waiting for me on the stove. Gideon wasn't in the house, but I sensed him nearby, sensed him in a way that hadn't been there before.

I texted Aeri, letting her know I wouldn't be in, and asked her to let me know if she had any trouble. She responded with a smile and a wink, which caused me to pause and wonder if there was any way she could know what had happened between Gideon and me the previous night.

I was certain there wasn't. But then again, my friends did have great insight.

I couldn't spot Gideon through the windows, so I quickly ate and dressed before I headed outside to find him.

I was disappointed that he wasn't in the immediate yard, and with so many trees surrounding us, it was hard to know where exactly he might be. So, I closed my eyes and slowly turned in a circle, using the soft tug in my heart to locate him. When I was certain I had the right direction, I opened my eyes and smiled.

I'm coming, I thought, and wondered if he'd hear me.

I followed a slender trail past a riot of yellow Leopard's Bane and clusters of Indian Paintbrush with orange spikes reaching for the heavens. The path took me across uneven terrain, into the trees, and up a slight incline. As I walked, I breathed deeply of the sweet mountain air. The sensation of him in my heart grew stronger, so much so that when I emerged into a clearing and found him with his hands in the dirt, my heart nearly burst with happiness.

He lifted his gaze, a brilliant smile on his face. "Good morning, lovely Daisy."

I strode toward him, and he stood. I gazed into his deep blue eyes, humbled by the fact that I could bring another so much joy. "It is a good morning. A very good morning, indeed."

He chuckled and bent his head to kiss me.

I accepted his offering and all the lovely sensations that came with it.

Afterward, he studied my eyes. "No regrets?"

His question brought a smile to my face. "None."

But I noticed that he didn't hug me, and I pulled back to glance at his dirt-covered hands. "What are you doing here?"

He grinned. "It's a secret garden. For you."

I glanced about, noticing rocks that had been piled to the side, and the rich, fertile soil that he'd uncovered. He already had a few plants in the ground, and I spied many more containers beyond the rocks.

He waved a hand, encompassing the area. "For your plants and herbs, and all the flowers that you love."

He couldn't have been more adorable. "How do you know which flowers I love?"

He shrugged. "You love them all, don't you?"

I laughed then, feeling freer than I ever had. "I suppose you're right."

He gestured to a cluster of potted plants waiting to be put in the ground. "I did choose a few pink dianthus on purpose, though."

I smiled and nodded. "For magic."

He agreed with a grin. "For magic and love."

He lifted his brow which stoked the fires inside me. "Would you like to help me finish planting these?"

I couldn't imagine anything better. "Absolutely. Aeri won't be expecting me, which gives me plenty of time to spend with you today."

A spark flashed in his eyes. "Perfect. After this, I'll show you the lovely pond that's not far from here. Should these plants require extra water, there's a nearby source that will work well with your magic."

I took his face into my hands and kissed him. Jocelyn had been wrong about Gideon. My heart would have known otherwise.

Midsummer. Litha. The perfect time to pick a new direction in life if a person needed one. Yes, I'd chosen a new path all right. Not the one that she'd wanted, but the perfect one for me.

FOURTEEN

The next day, I was still emotionally raw from my mom's and Jocelyn's antics. At least at my café, I had the support of my friends, and they weren't worried that Gideon had his sights set on my soul. I did my best to purge the residual anger smoldering inside me by cleaning during quiet times. My current project was the large window that looked out onto the town's charming Main Street.

Rosy pink petunias brightened pots along the sidewalk while the huge yellow-green leaves of sweet potato vines dripped down the sides. Dark clouds hung overhead, mirroring my current thoughts, and I suspected monsoon rains would arrive sooner than later that afternoon.

Still, I was hesitant to involve myself in the murder case, but I suspected that Gideon was right about the Goddess envisioning this path for me. I mean, I did find it interesting, but I'd worried I was inviting too much death into my life. Of course, living with a demon had brought more of that than anything else. He dealt with death every day and managed.

If this was what the Goddess wanted, then I supposed I could, too. I did find fulfillment in solving Merry's murder, and the experience of helping Herman Huber pass into the afterlife had been both frightening and beyond amazing. Maybe this was my gift. Maybe I should accept the calling and do what I could for others.

I squirted cleaner on the window and then froze. None other than Sailor Strickland walked past at that moment. That had to be a sign. It was far too coincidental otherwise.

I dropped the bottle of window cleaner and my rag to the corner of the floor and pushed them behind a potted palm with the toe of my shoe. I tapped the counter as I walked past to catch Aeri's attention. "Be right back."

Gusts of warm wind and the scent of rain in the air added to my prediction that it would storm before the afternoon was over. I hurried to catch up with Sailor, hoping to have enough time to talk to her before the heavens opened.

When I was close enough, I called out her name, and she turned back to look in my direction. She caught sight of me, frowned, and turned away. I groaned, knowing this would not be an easy conversation.

I filled my lungs with the humid air and hurried forward. "Sailor, wait. Give me just a minute, please."

She stopped then but didn't turn around, forcing me to walk past her and turn in order to face her.

The wind tossed her glossy brown hair about her face as she folded her arms across the faded blue Gucci t-shirt she wore. She met my gaze, and I found sadness and mistrust in her dark brown eyes. "What do you want?"

I lifted a hand in a show of peace. "I just wanted to apologize to you. I never would have blurted out the information about your mom if I'd recognized you. I've only ever seen you from a distance, and with your hair different, I didn't know who you were. I'm so sorry to have delivered the news that way."

She studied my face, and I sensed she was searching for sincerity. Then she shrugged. "What's done is done."

She spoke in a dull tone, as if there was nothing anyone could do to hurt her further.

A raindrop landed on her cheek, and then another splattered on my arm. We both glanced upward as more pelted down. I wasn't finished talking with her, but we couldn't stand in the pouring rain, either. "If you have a minute, why don't you come back to my café? I'll get you a coffee, and you can wait out the storm. These summer ones never last long."

Her hesitation was obvious from her expression, but then her shoulders relaxed. "Just until the storm lets up."

We both made a dash for Meowkins, and I held the door open for her. "We can sit out here or go into the Purry Parlor."

A hint of a smile tipped the corners of her mouth. "Purry Parlor. I've always wanted to see what it's like."

I smiled at her response. "It really is a cool place. Tell me your drink preference, and you can wait for me there."

"Vanilla Latte, iced."

I nodded. "Good choice. It's one of my most popular drinks. Head on in, and I'll be there in a minute."

As I walked behind the counter, Aeri regarded me with suspicion. "Is that Sailor Strickland?"

I grabbed a large plastic cup from the stack and added ice. "It is."

She snorted. "I thought you were staying out of the investigation."

I tamped the coffee grounds for espresso. "Apparently, that's not in the cards. Gideon thinks that the Goddess has chosen this path for me, and it's hard to argue with his logic since it's constantly been thrown in my face."

Aeri worked to steam the milk for Sailor's latte. "Honestly, it makes a lot of sense. Maybe that's why you were placed over peace and prosperity in the coven, too."

I shot her a doubtful look. "That's if Jocelyn doesn't change her mind any moment now and kicks me out."

She placed a reassuring hand on my arm. "You've gotta have faith, Miss Daisy Mae. Trust your heart, and trust the Goddess."

Once finished, I poured the espresso over ice, added vanilla syrup, and Aeri poured the steamed milk. She lifted her brows. "Whipped cream?"

I thought of Sailor and then nodded. "Yeah, give her whipped cream."

When I entered the Purry Parlor, I found Nicole and Sailor on the couch. My salt and pepper tabby kitty occupied Nicole's lap, and Sailor had my large orange tabby curled against her, languishing as Sailor stroked him from head to tail. I smiled. "Oh, Friskers loves that, doesn't he?"

Sailor glanced up at me with a proud smile. "He's purring a lot."

I caught Nicole's gaze and then glanced toward the door.

Nicole, who could read me as well as Aeri could, stood and set Mischief on the ground. "I'm going to step out for a quick break and give you two some privacy."

I approached Sailor and held out the vanilla latte to her.

She lifted a hand from Friskers and took the cup, and I noted that her movements didn't bother him in the least.

I sat next to her and scratched him between his ears. "He's a good boy. Very gentle and loving most of the time, but he does have his playful moments."

She sipped and then nodded. "I think I love him already."

I searched her energy for signs of a spoiled brat, as Liza had suggested, but the person in front of me came across as kind and gentle. Of course, master manipulators could often disguise themselves. "Are you doing okay? You know, with everything?"

She took a long moment to answer. "I guess. I mean, it's really hard not having my mom around."

"I can only imagine. Even though my mom isn't currently speaking to me, at least she's here."

Sailor looked at me from beneath her brows. "I sometimes fought with my mom, too. And now I regret every bit of it."

I gave her a kind smile. "I know. Hindsight can surely be a beast. But we're all going to have those moments in our lives, you know? You can't live with someone and not have a difference of opinion sometimes."

She pulled a tissue from the nearby table and dabbed at her nose. "I just worry that she didn't know how much I loved her."

"I'm sure she did. Even though you argued, you still loved her, right?"

She nodded.

"It was the same with your mom, I'm sure. Let your heart rest with that knowledge."

Sailor focused on Friskers, scratching behind his ears.

I was hesitant to broach the investigation, especially since she hadn't mentioned the murder or finding the perpetrator at all. But other than ensuring she was doing okay, that had been the point of me inviting her to the shop. "I suppose the police have already questioned you. Likely Alisha, too, since she lives on your property."

She blinked, looking bewildered. "Yeah. It was awful."

"How come?" I asked gently.

She scoffed. "They had the nerve to ask where we were that night. As if I might have done something to my mom."

I worked to keep my expression passive. "They're just doing their job, marking all the boxes. And I'm sure you had an alibi, right? Someone who could prove you weren't anywhere near the studio."

"Alisha and I were both home, both studying for a test we have coming up."

I drew my brows together. "I thought school was out for the summer."

In fact, I knew that it was.

"Yeah, but this is for an online class. It'll give us college credit, and then we won't have to take so many classes once we start in the fall. We both really want to finish early."

That was admirable. "So, you were studying together?"

She nodded. "Well, at the same time. She was at her house, and I was at mine. But we texted each other a lot, and I could see the lights on at her place."

She took a drink of her latte and set it on the table next to her. Then she put Friskers on my lap and reached into her bag. She produced a cell phone, tapped on it a few times, and then held it out for my inspection. "See. We were talking about our Sociology class."

I grimaced. "Not one of my favorite subjects."

She smiled then. "Mine, either."

I lifted a casual shoulder and let it drop. "Why didn't you guys just study together? Wouldn't that have been easier than constantly texting?"

"I don't know. We usually do, but Alisha didn't feel like it that night."

Which meant the girls had an alibi, of sorts. If they weren't together, it wasn't as solid. Still, so far, Sailor didn't seem like the spoiled, partying brat that Liza had made her out to be. "I hope you guys don't spend all your time studying. You need to make time for fun, too. You know, hang out with other friends and such."

"We do. If Alisha has the money, we go to the movies. I pay her way some of the time, too."

"That's really nice of you. It sounds like she and her mom struggle with finances."

"Yeah, they do. But Bobbi works really hard, and Alisha is really smart. I'm sure that once she finishes college, she'll be able to get a great job, and that will help her mom."

"Any idea what will happen with Bobbi now that your mom's gone?"

Her sadness deepened. "I don't know. I want her to be able to stay here. I'm almost eighteen, and that's considered an adult, so it's not like I couldn't have a house. My dad wants me to go live with him, but I don't want to sell my mom's. I have a lot of good memories there."

"But you'll have to pay utilities and taxes on the house, not to mention Bobbi's salary if she stays on. That's hard without a job."

She looked at me as though I'd betrayed her. "I'll get money from my mom's estate. Lots of it. I don't need to depend on my dad or anyone else. I'm tired of people trying to run my life. I can make my own decisions and take care of myself."

I leaned back as if to assure her that I wasn't challenging her decisions. "I'm sure you're quite capable, and there's no reason you have to decide what to do right this minute, either. Give yourself a chance to grieve first."

Her shoulders sagged as the fire inside her dimmed. "Yeah. I have too much to think about right now, anyway."

I nodded in understanding. "I'm curious what your impression is of Justin. Was he good to your mom?"

She hesitated a moment before she spoke. "I guess so. They seemed to like each other."

"Do you get along with him?"

She shrugged. "Yeah. I mean, I don't see him or talk to him much. But he's okay."

"You don't think he'd do anything to her, then?"

Sailor looked at me with a horrified expression. *"Like kill her?"*

I widened my eyes in curiosity. "Well, someone did. I'm just trying to figure out who."

She shook her head vehemently. "I don't know. A stranger? Maybe someone was trying to rob her? She has money in her office that someone might go after. But whoever did it is not anyone I know."

Her reaction caused me to wonder if my question had pushed her mental boundaries and if she couldn't accept that she might know the person who'd killed her mom.

Or perhaps, she hoped the police would think the murderer was a stranger, too, and not look too closely in her direction. Though I was leaning more toward her emotional instability.

I lifted Friskers. "Would you like to hold him a little longer? There's nothing like a kitty's purr to soothe the soul."

She shook her head and stood. "No. I need to go."

I gave the sweet cat a soft kiss on the head and set him on the floor before I stood. "Okay. Thanks for talking with me. If you ever want to come back and visit the cats, you're always welcome. They love the company."

Her demeanor softened, and she grabbed her latte. "I might do that. Thanks."

I walked her to the front door and found that the rain had indeed been short-lived. Not only that, but a brilliant rainbow hovered in the sky, shining bright against the dark clouds that were moving away.

Was the rainbow another sign? I wasn't sure.

When I turned back toward Aeri, she sent me an apprehensive look. "What?" I asked.

She sighed and shook her head. "Your mom just called me."

That surprised me. "She did. What did she say?"

"She tried to get me to intervene and help save your soul."

I gaped at her. "Seriously? Why can't she trust me?"

Aeri held her hands wide. "Don't know. But she now thinks I've been compromised as well."

I glanced to where Nicole sat at a table with her feet up on the opposing chair as she tapped out something on her phone. Then I turned back to Aeri. "Great Goddess. Pretty soon, she'll think Gideon has conned half the town."

One thing had become very clear that day. Time on earth could be very short. My mom was still fairly healthy, but there was no guarantee how long I'd have her, and I didn't want to be like Sailor, battling with regrets. I needed to talk to my mother, to beg her to see things as they really were. But that wouldn't be easy.

I groaned and stood, tackling first things first. "Guess I'd better warn Nicole that my mom is likely to call her next."

FIFTEEN

L ate that afternoon, I turned the corner into the next aisle at the grocery store and found Corey wearing street clothes, studying the bottle he held in his hand. The man looked good in jeans and a baggy t-shirt. Even out of uniform, he radiated confidence and strength.

I recalled the last conversation we'd had and smiled. He no longer intimidated me the way he had when he'd suddenly come back into my life, and I now considered him a friend. Even if he was a friend who'd made it clear that he was interested in something more.

I wheeled my cart toward him, and he looked up as I neared. A warm smile curved his lips and lit in his eyes. "Hey, Daisy."

I returned the gesture. "Whatcha got there?"

He lifted the bottle to show me. "I'm trying to find salad dressing that doesn't have a bunch of weird stuff in it. Trying to be healthier, you know?"

I scanned the selection, pulled down a bottle of my favorite Italian, and handed it to him. "I know. Me, too. My body would let me get away with eating all kinds of unhealthy stuff when I was younger, but no more."

He chuckled as he read the label. "Exactly." Then he dropped the bottle into his cart and met my gaze. "I'll give it a go."

I tried as hard as I could not to ask him about the case. And failed. "Anything new with your investigation?"

He lifted his shoulders and dropped them with a sigh. "Still chasing down leads. You were right about the exercise band being the murder weapon. No prints on it other than Liza's. And very few of those."

I considered that information. "That's not particularly helpful because it's unlikely that she'd be the only one to ever touch it, right? Unless it was brand new, the first time it had been held."

A pleased look glinted in his eyes. "That's right, and it's definitely not new."

"So, someone wiped it down, and then Liza touched it."

He tilted his head to the side and gave me a skeptical look. "There's the possibility that Liza could have wiped it down and then for some reason touched it afterward. Maybe she'd meant to wipe it clean again after she'd made the call."

He could be right. "Or perhaps Liza might have come to the conclusion we just did, thinking that holding the weapon with only her prints would make it seem like she was innocent."

He smiled again. "Good point."

I shifted my stance as I pondered the evidence. "Then basically, knowing it's the murder weapon doesn't help."

"Basically."

"I talked to Sailor Strickland yesterday. After what Liza had said about her, I wanted to get a feel for her."

"And," he said.

I smiled. "And she said you'd already interviewed her, so you know her alibi."

He chuckled. "I do. But I'm more interested in what your gut said about Sailor."

The thrill of being valued washed over me. "Sailor seemed genuinely sad, but when I brought up how Bobbi and Alisha would manage without the income from cleaning Karyn's house, she became defensive. She complained that her dad wanted to sell it, that she wanted to stay, and that she'd inherit a lot of money from her mom, enough to do what she wanted."

He nodded slowly. "All of that is true, though."

I dug deep and tried to pinpoint the source of my concern. "It wasn't so much as what she said, but the way she said it, I think. She said she was tired of people trying to run her life, and it didn't seem like she meant only since her mom's death."

"Well, she is at that age of emerging independence. I would expect having the finances to back up her words makes her feel powerful. In control, where not much would be these days."

I smiled at his summation of her. "That's a lot of insight into her psyche for someone who asks others for their opinion."

He chuckled. "I have insight, the kind you have to study and develop. Not the magical kind like yours. It's different."

The sound of a woman calling my name drew my gaze to the end of the aisle. Bobbi Knowles waved and hurried toward me. As she approached, I recognized her fear and desperation.

When she reached us, she dismissed Corey with a blink of her tired eyes and focused on me. "I saw your car in the parking lot. Can I talk to you?" She flicked another glance at Corey. "Alone?"

He gave me a knowing look and then turned to Bobbi. "I need to be on my way anyway. Good to talk to you Daisy. We'll catch up soon."

I figured that was his code for saying he'd leave me alone with her in the hopes that I might learn more. "Sounds good. I'll see you later."

Corey nodded to Bobbi and then sauntered away, glancing at the products on the shelves as he did.

I shifted my gaze to the harried-looking woman, wishing I had some news to share with her that might help her current living situation. "Everything okay?"

She clenched her jaw as tears welled in her eyes, and she shook her head. "No. Things are worse."

She stepped closer to me in a way that solidified my attention. "The police are now looking at my Alisha and at Sailor as suspects. What's wrong with this world? Those two are doing nothing but working hard on their studies. But word got out that the police questioned them. People are whispering. They think my girl could *commit murder*."

I took a small step back, increasing my personal space to a comfortable level. "I'm sure the police are just following every lead."

She shook her head vehemently. "No. They already questioned them both, asked for alibis the day after Karyn died. This was something more."

I had a feeling I knew who'd casted further suspicion on the girls. Liza. She was likely feeling the heat of the investigation. Likely wanted people to focus elsewhere. Not that I hadn't wondered about Sailor myself, though. "I'm sorry to hear that. It must be very worrisome."

Bobbi pierced me with a compelling gaze. "I want to hire you, Daisy. I know you've helped with other cases, and I want you to prove that my girl is innocent."

Her proposal caused the air to empty from my lungs in a surprised rush. "Oh, I'm not a private investigator or anything like that, Bobbi. I run a coffee shop, remember?"

She waved a hand between us. "I don't want a professional. I—I can't afford one. But I think you could help Alisha. She's innocent, Daisy. I need to protect her. She has her whole life ahead of her, and this could ruin everything."

If Alisha truly was innocent, I doubted the investigation would mess up her life, and rumors would fade after the culprit was found. But I could understand a mother's worries, even if they were unfounded. It didn't escape me that they were likely similar to my mother's where Gideon was concerned. "Okay. I can try, but I can't guarantee anything."

She jerked her head in the direction Corey had gone. "Talk to Corey. Let him know that Alisha is a good girl. A perfect girl."

I narrowed my gaze slightly. It was one thing to ask me to help investigate. Quite another to try to use my influence with friends on the police force. "I can talk to him, see if he can give me an idea of how strongly he feels about her as a suspect, but he's not going to stop his investigation on my behalf. He has to do his job, Bobbi."

She buried her face in her hands, then wiped tears from her cheeks. "I'm desperate, Daisy. Please help me."

I nodded solemnly. "I'll do what I can, okay? I'll focus on looking for clues that might help find the killer. Once they have a person in custody, it will exonerate Alisha."

Bobbi drew her fingers up and down the side of her face. "I guess. Just, please, do what you can."

She glanced down the aisle again. "I need to go. I'm supposed to be at the studio cleaning before the afternoon yoga class starts."

I did my best to give her a reassuring smile, and then she turned and strode away. I knew I hadn't told her what she'd wanted to hear, but short of casting a disillusion spell on Corey, which would net me a whole lot of negative Karma, there wasn't much else I could do.

SIXTEEN

I returned from the grocery store and was happy to find Gideon's black Mercedes parked in the driveway. He'd been called away so often lately, that it left me wondering if things were worse than I'd imagined.

But he was here now, and that's what mattered.

That and the fact that he could help me carry in the groceries, I thought with a smile.

No sooner had I opened my door than Gideon emerged from the house, looking casually comfortable in jeans and a light-weight blue sweater.

I met his gaze, and a warm, sensual smile curved his lips. I'd never get tired of that look, of seeing how my presence would light up his eyes. It didn't matter what my mother or Jocelyn thought of him. He was the man for me. "Help with the groceries?"

He reached me, lightly placed a hand on my shoulder, before he drew his fingertips down my arm, leaving me with a frisson of shivers. "Anything for you, my lovely."

I laughed. "Leave it to you to put the sexy in hauling in groceries."

A hint of dark flashed in his eyes, and he arched his brow. "Do I now?"

I chuckled as I grabbed sacks from the trunk, but by the time we'd reached the front door, my mood had grown serious. In the kitchen,

I placed bags on the counter and met his gaze as he did the same. "You're not headed out, immediately, are you?"

He gave a slight shake of his head. "No, why?"

I pulled items out of the bag in front of me. "It seems as if your work has needed you more often recently. I want your opinion on something, but it might take a little time."

He stopped unloading groceries and focused on me. "I'm here all evening. I've really enjoyed our quiet time together and wanted more. So, I told them I would be unavailable."

The thought of our beautiful nights together relaxed me in a way that little else could. "Good. Let's get this stuff put away, and I'll make us tea."

We'd finished the chore and sat on the overstuffed light-gray couch in our cozy living room, both holding mugs of hibiscus lemon tea. I glanced beyond him, to the view of pines and wildflowers surrounding our sanctuary and reminded myself again how lucky I was to have him in my life.

Not only did I have a beautiful place to live, but he'd coaxed me from a shallow existence, and my life had improved in so many ways.

Though I wasn't certain about the one issue currently on my mind.

He drew my gaze back to him with the tip of his finger. "So pensive. What troubles you? Your mother?"

I sighed. "Well, her, too. When my feet feel solid beneath me, I'll stop by and see what I can do to mend things between us. If I take her favorite linguini and vegetables from Deliziosa, she'll have to let me in."

He smiled. "A joke is good. It helps with healing, though I know how much this troubles you. I'm sorry for that."

I shook my head. "No. You will not be sorry for being the best thing in my life."

Freya lifted her head, focused yellow eyes on me, and meowed her complaint about not being the favorite.

I snorted. "Oh, look at you," I said to her. "You complain, but in case you haven't noticed, you're snuggled up to him and not me."

Gideon chuckled and stroked her gorgeous gray fur. "She loves me. Maybe more than you.".

Freya glanced between us and then stood. As she made her way from his lap to mine, I lifted a hand. "We're just teasing. You don't need to move."

But my familiar continued until she sat squarely on my lap and then sank down into a purring loaf. I grinned at her silliness. "We can all love more than one soul, Freya."

Gideon met my gaze with an unreadable emotion in his eyes.

I took that moment to reach out to him, to place my hand on his firm jawline. "I'll deal with my mom. Once she meets you, I have no doubt she'll like you, too."

He nodded, though I sensed the unsettled emotions inside him. "If it's not your mother, then what?"

I sipped my tea, allowing my mind a chance to shift gears. "As you know, my life is almost completely different than what it was only a few short months ago."

He lifted his brow. "It suits you."

I couldn't deny that. "I know. It's just that between moving houses, taking on coven duties, and being involved in two murder investigations, I haven't had much time for adjustment."

He gave a brief nod of acknowledgement.

"We have a new life. I'd been worried about telling my mom about us, which blew up in my face, and the high priestess of my coven isn't super happy with me, either. I've been trying hard to stay away from the Strickland murder investigation, but every time I turn around, it seems I'm being sucked back in. By my own actions or someone else's. So, I've been considering what you said about this being the path the Goddess chose for me."

He lifted his head in a knowing gesture. "You believe me now?"

I shrugged. "Maybe. I just wanted to talk it through again."

He smiled but remained silent, waiting for me to continue.

"My friends think the Goddess has called me to help, too. Even Corey forced me to participate in a witness questioning and then when I saw him this afternoon, he was interested in my perceptions of suspects."

Both brows rose this time. "You saw Corey today?"

I smiled. Gideon's jealousy of Corey warmed my heart. But then I remembered how I'd felt when Vivian had flirted relentlessly with Gideon and sobered. "Corey lives in this town, and you know as well as I do that Sweet Mountain Meadows isn't that big. He's in charge of the investigation and will likely be of others in the future. If I try to help the hands of justice, I can't completely avoid him."

He exhaled a weighted sigh. "I cannot love you and then deny you your passion, can I?"

"You could."

He shook his head. "Not if I love you."

I loved him for that. "But I'm torn. I feel like I need to focus on you. On our relationship. On the cats. My job. My mom."

He drew his brows together. "And you feel this leaves you with nothing left to give to anything else?"

I narrowed my gaze and pondered his question. "I don't know. My heart is with you, with my family, but my thoughts constantly turn elsewhere. Just today, Bobbi Knowles asked me to help prove her daughter's innocence. And I want to do it. I want to find the answers. But investigating, poking my nose into other people's business seems to bring a lot of drama. Drama that I'm not sure I should encourage."

"It's obviously something you love, or you'd be able to turn away. It calls to your heart. That shouldn't be ignored."

He hesitated for a moment before speaking again. "Perhaps you need to view things differently. Instead of drama, consider it trading energy for information. You don't hesitate to pay for things that you want like the groceries you brought home. Nor do you hesitate to put effort into your café to make it a pleasant experience for those who come in."

I nodded slowly as his words began to make sense. "So, this is just a different kind of exchange? Accepting uncomfortable situations, even confrontations, to gain the final product, the solving of the mystery?"

He smiled with approval. "How does it feel now, through that lens?"

I grinned. "Good. It feels good. It seems like the perfect way for me to help people and feed my love of intrigue. Are you sure you're okay with that? With me being around Corey? I swear on all that's dear to me that he's nothing more than a friend."

He focused piercing eyes on me. "But would he be more if I wasn't here?"

I shrugged, because I really didn't know the answer to his question, and then took his hand. "I'm here with you, Gideon. *This* is where I want to be. *You're* who I want to be with. I can't say what life would be like if you weren't here, and I never want to know, either."

Potent energy circled between us, and I sensed the ease in his heart.

He assured me with a nod. "I'll be fine as long as I have your heart."

I drew my fingertips across the short hair near his ear, thinking of how he'd made things so simple. "This is one of the many reasons that I love you."

All energy in the room ceased to move, and the dark look in Gideon's eyes stole my breath. His voice was low and deceptively soft when he spoke. "Do not toss those words around carelessly, Daisy. I beg of you."

Dear Goddess. Without realizing it, I'd proclaimed my love for him. I steadied my gaze and spoke with the reverence the moment required. "I don't. I said it, and I meant it."

Something warm and powerful encircled my heart. "I love you, Gideon. I love everything about you, whether you believe I can or not."

A hesitant smile blossomed on his face. He set his mug on the coffee table and then did the same with mine. Without regard to Freya, who jumped from my lap, he pulled me into his arms and gifted me with a long, slow kiss. "I love you, too, my Daisy. I can't imagine a life where I wouldn't."

SEVENTEEN

Gideon's phone had rung multiple times over the past hour and a half, but he'd insisted on ignoring the calls. It wasn't until after we'd feasted on a delicious meal of baked chicken and asparagus that black ravens began tapping at the windows with their beaks, and he finally relented.

He splayed a hand across his heart. "Please forgive me, Daisy."

I shrugged, not wanting him to feel bad. "Go ahead and answer. It's obviously something important."

He snatched his phone from where it sat on the kitchen table and headed out the back door to the cobblestone patio. I tried not to invade his privacy, but it was hard not to glance at him every now and again as he paced across the stones. He seemed angry. And then resigned.

A moment later, he stepped back inside, and I dropped my gaze to the counter that I had been wiping down. When the door shut firmly, I looked at him. "Everything okay?"

He released a heavy sigh, and I could see the self-disappointment in his eyes. "I'm needed. I'm so sorry."

I strode to him, wrapped my arms around his waist. "Don't be. I know you're important and that your working hours are not like most of the rest of us. You go. I'll be here waiting when you get home."

He placed a warm kiss on my lips. "Don't wait up for me, okay? I might be a while."

I did my best to smile. "I'll try not to."

The moment he strode out the door, I knew I'd go insane if I sat home and fretted. With the midsummer solstice almost upon us, the sun would be burning in the sky for several more hours, and I needed to find something to distract me. I could focus on investigating for Bobbi, but the rift between my mother and me weighed heavy on my heart. I had to try again to make her see reason.

I thought about calling ahead to let her know I'd be stopping by, but she might try to concoct a spell that would...I don't know...erase my memory? One that would keep me locked in her basement? Who knew what a desperate mom might do to try to protect her daughter? Even if I was forty years old.

A bright orange sun hung low on the horizon as I parked at my mother's quaint and cozy house. Bright purple delphiniums and cheerful sunflowers bloomed in her gardens just the same as they did every summer, reminding me that the wheel of the year would always turn, and that life, despite the bumps in the road I currently experienced, would go on.

Though I didn't usually ring the doorbell at her house, I did give a quick knock to let her know I was there and then entered.

My mom was halfway between the kitchen and the front door, hurrying toward me faster than I'd seen her move in the months since her surgery.

I hadn't been sure what kind of reception I'd get after the way I'd left the last time I'd visited, but it definitely wasn't her racing toward me with outstretched arms.

"Daisy. Oh, Daisy. You've come back to me."

Despite the look of shock on my face, she embraced me with a warm hug.

I embraced her in return because I always did with my mom, inhaled the scent of her familiar perfume, and then pushed back. "Mum. Please, stop with the dramatics."

She released me and shook her head as happy tears gathered in the corners of her eyes. "But you're okay, Daisy. I can sense that you're still my girl and that nothing bad has happened."

I snorted and took her hand in mine. "Let's go sit down, okay?"

She let me lead her into her sitting room, and I side-eyed her magical chest as we passed it. Once she was settled comfortably in her chair and me on the couch near her, I focused on her with a stern gaze. "You're right, Mum. I am completely fine. In fact, I'm the happiest I've been since I can remember."

She narrowed her gaze, and a look of suspicion replaced her happiness. "Don't fall for his tactics, Daisy. I know what you're experiencing might feel real, but it's not."

A laugh bubbled out of me at her comment. "Of course, it is. Look, I understand that you have a problem with demons. I get that. Before I met Gideon, I felt the same. Everything I'd ever heard about them was bad, but we were wrong, Mum. Gideon is one of the kindest people I know."

She turned her head away from me, looking out her large window to the picturesque mountains that towered above our little town. "Don't try to convince me. I know what I know."

"Do you know Gideon?" I asked softly.

She glanced back at me then. "I don't need to."

I sent her a puzzled look. "Then how can you know what kind of person he is?"

"He's not a person. He's a *demon*."

I did my best to resist rolling my eyes. "He is a person, Mum. He has a soul just like we do. The only thing different is his job."

She scoffed. *"His job?"*

I paused to settle my emotions before we ended up in a situation like we had the last time during her and Jocelyn's so-called intervention. "Let me put it this way. The Goddess, she likes balance in all things, right?"

My mother begrudgingly nodded.

"Light balanced with dark keeps the wheel turning. The Goddess gave us all our freedom of choice. If we make good ones, we keep the light burning bright inside us. If not, Karma plays a role. If someone chooses to do something really bad, they'll need to relinquish their soul in exchange. But it's still a choice, Mum. People like Gideon make those options possible and keep us accountable."

She stared at me for a long moment, and I wondered if I might have gotten through to her. Then she shook her head. "Those are all pretty words, Daisy. Is that something Gideon said to convince you?"

Frustration welled up. "He did say something similar to me, but that was after my heart saw his, after I recognized the goodness in him."

"There is no goodness in demons."

I shrugged. "Maybe not in some. I've only ever met him, but he has a good heart and a good soul. I've sensed both on so many occasions. You would, too, if you could find it in your heart to give him a chance."

Again, I thought she might consider my words, but then her features closed in, and she shook her head. "You don't know what I know, or you wouldn't be so gullible."

The urge to walk out burned bright, but I hunkered down. "Fine. Then tell me what you know. I can't possibly believe that it will change my mind, but I'm willing to listen."

She clamped her lips shut and shook her head. "I can't."

I threw my hands open wide. "This is ridiculous. I'm trying to bridge the gap that's between us, and you're being completely illogical. You say one thing, but you can't back it up, and you're not willing to give Gideon the tiniest bit of a chance."

I stood and paced. "I don't know, Mum. I never thought we'd find ourselves in this kind of a situation, but here we are. If we want out of it, you're going to have to give on one front or the other."

She stared at me for a long moment and then spoke quietly. "If I tell you, it will hurt you, and I don't want to do that."

I looked at her as if she was insane. "What do you think is happening right now? I love someone that you despise. That hurts."

Her hand flew to her throat, and she gasped. "No, Daisy. No. You can't love him."

I gave her a snarky blink. "Well, I do. He's the best man I've ever known, so kind to me, my kitties, and my friends, and I love him. So, there's that."

I dropped back onto the couch, folded my arms, and prepared to wait her out.

Ten minutes of stony silence passed before she quietly cleared her throat. When she spoke, all emotion that had colored her words was gone. "Fine. I'll tell you what you need to hear. And I'm sorry that it will break your heart. It was never my intention."

I turned to her with a blank expression.

She gave a small nod as though reassuring herself. "A demon killed your father, Daisy."

Her declaration whisked my thoughts into a tangled mess. "My father?"

"Yes. It was the most horrific tragedy that I've ever endured. I was there when the demon came. Your father was so scared. I was terrified, and you were screaming. I didn't think it could happen like that, but in an instant, your dad was gone."

Her words did indeed hurt me. "Oh, Mum. I'm so sorry."

Years of despair lined her face, and she shook her head repeatedly.

I went to her, knelt next to her chair, and took her cold hands into mine. "I don't know what kind of a deal my father made with that demon, but...and I know this will be hard to hear. But demons only collect the souls of those who've contracted with them. They don't randomly kill people."

She shook off my hands, angry. "Don't tell me lies. There was no reason your father would have willingly given up his soul."

She'd thought I'd be as wounded by her declaration as she'd been when she'd lost my dad. But I only had fleeting images of him and had never had the opportunity to connect deeply with him or see into his heart. I placed a hand on the arm of her chair to steady myself. "That's how it works, Mum."

She jerked her head back and forth. "I won't listen to the lies that the demon has put into your head."

I stood and found my way back to the couch. I watched her for a long moment until she finally met my gaze. "What do we do, then?" I asked softly. "I can't lose you or Gideon."

My mom searched my expression and then sighed. "And I won't lose you to him."

My heart *was* broken, but because of our situation. I dropped my shoulders. "He's not trying to take me away from you, Mum. He just wants a chance to meet you. I want that, too. I want you to see what I see, that he's a good man. A good person, and not his job."

She hesitated, and her expression crumpled. "I don't know that I could ever trust him. Don't know that I ever want to look at his face or into his heart to find out. I don't think I could trust myself, either, at that point. I...just don't know."

I begged the Goddess to show me another option but none came. "I guess we wait until you can, then."

The look in her eyes turned hopeful. "You could come live with me."

I shook my head. "I'm happy where I am. I'm with the person that's meant for me."

She drew her lips inward, and I knew that she held back her words. After a long moment, she stood. "Until one of us concedes, could you do something for me?"

"Of course. I'll do anything except sacrifice my happiness."

My mom strode to the small desk that sat near her chest and opened a drawer. From within, she retrieved a small blue pouch and then walked to me. She held it out by the strings that kept it closed. "Wear this."

I accepted her gift and opened the bag. A large black crystal attached to a thick silver chain, ripe with magic, fell into my hands. I lifted my gaze. "Obsidian?"

She released a weighted breath. "It will protect your soul. If anyone should try to harm you, to take your soul, it will burn hot to warn you. If this happens, you shouldn't hesitate to run."

I glanced at the stone. Perhaps this was the bridge between us. If I wore it and nothing bad happened to me, she would eventually see that she had nothing to fear from Gideon. "I will wear it on one condition. You can specify whatever amount of time you're comfortable with, but if I wear it for that long and you can see that I'm perfectly safe, you'll agree to meet Gideon. You don't have to love him, you don't have to stay long, but you must agree to meet him with an open heart. Deal?"

She twitched her lips as she pondered and then met my gaze. "Fine. It's going to kill me to wait, worrying every day if you're okay. But if he can remain good for three months, until Samhain, I'll meet him for a brief moment, just long enough to sense his heart."

Hope lit the smile on my face. "That's all I ask. I'll call or come see you all the time, like I always have, so you'll know that I'm fine."

She pulled me into a fierce hug. "Thank you. May the goddess bless and protect you, my daughter."

EIGHTEEN

It was dark by the time I left my mother's house, and I drove toward home with conflicted feelings. I was grateful that my mom and I had found a compromise of sorts, but I felt bad knowing that she would worry unnecessarily. Still, that couldn't be helped because I refused to give up one of the best things that had ever happened in my life.

I purposefully chose the path home that took me past the Expanding Universe. Classes would have ended a while ago and the chance that Justin might still be there was small, but I figured it was worth a try. Especially since Gideon wouldn't likely be home for a while.

The Goddess must have pitied me for the encounter with my mom because, as luck would have it, Justin's yellow Jeep was still parked at the studio's lot near the sidewalk. I slowed and pulled to the opposite side of the street, parking in the space between two houses, in the shadow of a large tree.

I considered going inside to talk to Justin. Unfortunately, no one else was around, and the thought of entering a building alone to confront someone stronger than me who may or may not have recently committed murder didn't seem like the best idea.

But I could wait for him to come out. I would have my magical pepper spray at the ready, and I could easily stand on the sidewalk in plain sight of anyone who might pass while I talked to him.

With that settled, I pulled out my phone to see if Gideon had messaged me. Unfortunately, he hadn't.

As a precaution, I sent a message to Nicole who wouldn't be busy with a husband and kids, just to let her know my plans to talk to Justin. She responded with a request to let her know when I'd finished my sleuthing and was safe.

I pocketed my phone and sighed. I supposed patience would be a requirement on a stakeout, and the knowledge that I was doing exactly that gave me a good dose of it.

While I waited, I considered everything I knew about Justin. Which wasn't much. He'd been Karyn's boyfriend, liked attention from the ladies, and he'd been in the workout studio the night of the murder. Sailor had seemed okay when I'd mentioned him. But Liza thought he should be a suspect.

Except Liza had said the same about everyone in Karyn's life. The only interactions I'd had with Justin was catching him kissing a woman that he shouldn't have and the look he'd given me the night of the murder.

Headlights approached from behind, and I watched in my rearview mirror until a sleek, black sedan passed me. Then, surprisingly, it turned into the studio's parking lot. When I recognized that it was the same model as Karyn's car, my instincts jumped to attention. What were the chances that it wasn't her car?

Slim to none.

The person didn't park near Justin's Jeep, which was in the area closest to the front door, but instead pulled to the far back corner of the parking lot where two large oaks shadowed it.

The headlights shut off, and I watched for someone to emerge. I figured the only people who possibly might drive Karyn's car were Bobbi or Sailor. Or perhaps her ex-husband Ian since the car now belonged to Sailor but he was her legal guardian.

Unfortunately, no one immediately emerged.

I, myself, had parked beneath a tree, away from streetlights, so that Justin wouldn't see me sitting in my car. Not that he'd have any reason to suspect I'd be targeting him that night. But obscurity was always good, I'd decided and was now proven right. Still, I wondered if whoever was in Karyn's car had noticed me.

Either way, I intended to be patient.

Another five minutes passed before movement at the front door caught my eye. Justin emerged, wearing the only thing I'd ever seen him in, a black tank top that showcased his massive arms and gray jogger pants. He paused to lock the door behind him and then strolled down the sidewalk toward his car.

Indecision tore at me. This was my chance to question him, but if I did, then I'd never know what the person driving Karyn's car was up to. I reached for the door handle once, then twice, and then growled my frustration as I sank against the seat.

When Justin pulled onto the street, I ducked so that his headlights wouldn't illuminate me as he passed. Hopefully, he'd assumed that my car belonged to the people at the closest house, if he'd even noticed me at all.

When the interior of my car darkened once again, I lifted to a sitting position and studied the black car hidden in the shadows. Minutes ticked by, increasing my anxiety, making me wonder if the person behind the wheel was waiting to see what I did, just as I waited for the same.

Then the interior of the car lit for a moment as the door opened before it went dark again. I strained to see who'd emerged and caught sight of a short, slender person hurrying toward the studio. Based on body size, I guessed it was Sailor, but I couldn't be sure because whoever it was wore a dark jacket with the hood up.

Still, the person hadn't wanted to be seen, which ratcheted up my curiosity immensely.

When the person approached a side entrance and a small tree blocked my view, I hurried and slipped from my car.

I strode until I was centered with the building to hide me from view and dashed across the street. Cautiously, I crept along the bushes in front and paused when I reached the side of the building, listening for noises that might let me know if the person was still outside or if she'd entered.

The sound of glass shattering echoed through the quiet night, and I clamped my hand over my mouth to keep from gasping. Whoever it was must not have had a key, which kept me thinking it was Sailor. Bobbi would no doubt have one because she needed early and late access. And the person was too short to be Sailor's father.

The only other person who might have access to Karyn's car would be Alisha. Though I couldn't imagine why she'd want to break into the building after hours. Honestly, I had no idea why any of them would, but I was eager to find out.

I stayed low as I crept next to the bushes that grew alongside the building and paused before I reached the doorway. When I heard no further sounds, I took a quick peek and found the area deserted.

I cautiously stepped forward until I spied a broken side window near the door handle. Glass at my feet sparkled from the overhead light.

With my pepper spray in hand, I quietly stepped over the broken glass, tugged open the door, and stepped inside.

The hallways were mostly dark like they had been after my first class, with only residual light coming from the reception area. I paused to survey my surroundings but couldn't see any movement. With the way clear, I tiptoed forward with all my senses open and listened for signs of life. A sound that seemed like a filing cabinet drawer shutting echoed from a distance and gave me courage to increase my pace.

A few moments later, the sound repeated, and I realized I'd reached the area where the women's locker rooms were. I knew how to get to Karyn's office from that point, and I suspected that I might find the black-clad woman there.

When I was only yards away from the office, I slowed as I moved forward, taking care not to make a sound. I reached the doorway, and, much like I had the night I'd discovered Liza standing over Karyn's body, I peeked inside.

At that point, I had no lingering doubts that the person was a woman even though she had her back to me. She must have sensed me, though, because she turned, and I found myself staring at Sailor Strickland's youthful face.

Guilt reddened her cheeks, and she quickly took a step backward, tucking something that looked like an envelope behind her back.

"What are you doing here, Sailor?"

She must have regained her senses because she gaped at me and then snorted. "No. The question is, what are *you* doing here? This is my mom's studio, actually my studio now, so I don't have to explain myself."

I chuckled, giving her credit for her quick thinking. "Then why did you break in?"

She seemed stunned that I knew what she'd done and hesitated. "I forgot my key."

I lifted my brows in disbelief. "So, you broke the glass to get in as opposed to driving, what, less than five minutes back to your house?"

She clenched her jaw. "That's none of your business. I can do what I want. And you'd better leave before I call the cops and have you arrested for breaking and entering."

I shrugged. "Go ahead. I was planning to do the same myself, and we'll let the fine officers of Sweet Mountain Meadows sort things out."

Her jaw tightened, and she shook her head. "Just leave! This is my life. Stay out of it."

With my gaze trained on her, I slipped the phone from my pocket, and with a brief glance, dialed for emergency services and let them know to send officers in through the side door.

Rage radiated from her, and the second I ended the call, she ran toward me. I lifted a hand and spewed a spell that I hadn't used since grade school when my cousin Merry had bullied me.

With no magical protection of her own, Sailor stumbled backward and fell into her mother's white leather office chair. She seemed stunned, and I took the opportunity to warn her. "You'll stay right where you are until the police arrive."

Fear brought tears to her eyes, and she stared at me with hatred.

We stayed like that until the police entered the building.

"Back here," I called, and I admit a small measure of relief washed over me when Officer Sofia Doyle approached.

She took one look at me, then inside the office at Sailor, and holstered her gun. We waited while she pressed the mic on her shoulder radio to notify someone of the circumstances. Then she shifted her gaze between the two of us. "We received a call of breaking and entering."

Sailor pointed a sharp finger at me. "Arrest her. She has no right to be in this building."

Officer Doyle regarded Sailor. "And you are?"

"Sailor Strickland. My father and I now own this studio."

Sofia arched her brow at me.

I smiled. "That's all well and true, but Sailor won't receive ownership until she turns eighteen. Or later, depending on her mother's will. Plus, I just witnessed her, dressed in all black like a thief might be, break a window near the side door to get into the building. Then I found her rifling through her mother's filing cabinets. I think she might have discovered what she was looking for because she has something hidden in her hands. I wonder if it might have something to do with her mother's death."

Sailor glared at me.

Sofia turned to her. "Is this true? You broke a window to get in?"

She shrugged. "I can do what I want."

Sofia gave her a small nod. "Show me what you have in your hands."

The sound of something hitting the floor behind the desk was obvious, and Sailor held her empty hands outward.

Sofia gestured with a curve of her fingers. "Both of you, please come into the hall."

I exited and found Officer Kemp waiting. Sailor appeared a few seconds later, sulking as she did what she was told. Sofia nodded her approval. "Stay here."

Sofia reentered the office and a moment later reappeared. In her gloved hand, she held a white letter-sized envelope stuffed so full that the flap stuck out. "I found this on the floor near the chair. Care to tell me what's inside?"

Sailor only stared.

Sofia gave the teenager a smile that said she'd dealt with obstinance before. "No worries. I'll have a look for myself."

She lifted the flap, and I could see the stack of money from where I stood. "Hmm... This is interesting," she said and looked at Sailor. "Care to explain?"

Sailor sent her a saucy look. "I'd like to call my lawyer."

Officer Kemp sighed. "That can be arranged. We'll need you both to come down to the station. You can come willingly, or we'll cuff you."

"Willingly," I offered.

"Fine," Sailor snarled.

I led the way out to the police car and climbed into the backseat. Officer Kemp opened the opposite door, and Sailor dropped onto the seat next to me with a huff. When the doors were closed, she muttered at me. "You have no idea what you've done."

I supposed not, but I'd wager a bet that I was about to find out.

NINETEEN

When we arrived at the police station, Officer Kemp guided Sailor to an interview room, promising that she could call her attorney. Sofia led me to a similar one across the hall. She closed the door behind her and pointed to a chair. "Have a seat."

Normally when she and I interacted it was with me behind the counter at Meowkins serving her coffee, so this all felt bizarre to me. She claimed the chair on the opposite side of the table and pulled out a small notebook. "Tell me what happened, from beginning to end, and don't leave anything out."

I thought of asking to speak to Corey instead because he would understand why I was sitting outside of the Expanding Universe in the first place, waiting for Justin. But I supposed that I had a legitimate enough reason if I told Sofia that Bobbi had asked me to help clear her daughter.

Sofia listened and took notes as I went through each detail, omitting, of course, when I'd used a spell to stop Sailor from leaving, and then she regarded me with a frown. "You do realize that what you did was dangerous, correct? Not to mention, you didn't legally have a right to be inside the studio after hours."

I gave her a small smile and shrugged. "Technically, I'm a patron of the Expanding Universe, and the door wasn't locked."

She snorted and shook her head. "That doesn't give you after-hours access. If Ian Strickland wants to press charges, good luck telling that to the judge."

She continued jotting notes, and I tried to read her messy handwriting upside down from across the table. "You know as well as I do that Sailor was doing something she shouldn't. If I would have waited for the police to arrive, who knows what might have happened."

Sofia closed her notebook, sent me a scolding look, and stood.

I gazed at her with questioning eyes. "Am I free to go?"

"Not yet. Go ahead and relax where you are. I may have further questions."

"Oh. After you compare my statement to what Sailor told Officer Kemp."

Instead of commenting, Sofia only smiled and exited the room, closing the door behind her. I considered testing it to see if she'd locked it.

Before I could, the door opened again, and Corey strode in looking confidently handsome in his uniform. "Come with me."

The lack of friendliness in his voice worried me, but I followed him to his office. I took a seat as he suggested, and he closed the door behind us.

Once he was seated across from me, he met my gaze and sighed. "When I encouraged you to talk to people and see if you could get a sense for the truth, I didn't mean that you should go sneaking around at night, breaking into buildings, and confronting possible felons."

I raised my eyebrows in excitement. "So, Sailor was doing something she shouldn't. How much money was in that envelope?"

He exhaled his disappointment and shook his head. "Did you hear a word I just said?"

I frowned. "I wasn't sneaking up on a madman with a gun. It was only Sailor. She's much smaller than me, and I have...you know, things to help me protect myself."

He lifted a sardonic brow. "Like the spell you used to assault Sailor?"

I gasped. "Is that what she told you?"

Amusement twinkled in his eyes, and he admonished me with another shake of his head. "The point is, don't do something like this again."

I sank back against my chair. "Okay."

But he wasn't so easily swayed. "Promise me."

I hesitated.

"Promise me," he said more firmly.

"How can I promise when I don't know what the future holds? What if I accidentally find myself in that position again?"

The look in his eyes turned hard. "Then you'll call me."

Of course, I would call the police. I had that time, too, hadn't I? I didn't say it, but I'd been around the block enough times to know when I could handle something and when I couldn't. "Fine."

I sent him a disappointed frown. "I just helped prevent a crime, and you're not going to tell me anything?"

He considered me for a long moment and leaned back against his chair. "We haven't deemed it a crime yet. That all depends on her father."

I shook my head in disappointment. "If it was fine for her to take that money, she wouldn't have broken in."

"I agree with you, Daisy. But we'll need to see what Ian Strickland has to say first. Sailor said it was money for her tuition that her mom should have paid but hadn't. Said the deadline is tomorrow, and she didn't want to ask her dad or wait for him when she already knew where the money was."

I narrowed my gaze. "Sounds fishy to me. Why would Karyn have the funds for tuition sitting as cash in a drawer?"

He shrugged. "People are weird."

That was certainly true.

I waited for him to answer a call and then hang up before I spoke again. "Can I go home now?"

He stood. "Not yet."

I glared at him, thinking he wasn't as handsome as I'd first thought. "I'm tired, and I want to be home. You need to arrest me, or let me go."

He stopped at the door and glanced back. "Don't tempt me."

I folded my arms and exhaled my frustration. I'd done my duty. I shouldn't be punished for it. And I wanted to know how much money Sailor had taken. And why she'd had to break in to do it.

The door opened a few minutes later, and a tall man with silver shot through his dark hair, wearing a very nice suit, entered. I immediately recognized him from the photo behind the reception desk at the fitness studio.

"You can wait in my office," Corey said to him. "We'll let you know when you can see your daughter."

Corey closed the door behind him.

Ian Strickland took the chair next to mine and regarded me with a puzzled look. "Is there a reason that you're here?"

I supposed I could tell him that I was the reason his daughter was in custody, but decided that might not be the best decision. "I'm waiting for Sergeant Hancock, too."

He gave me a curt nod. Then pulled out his phone and began to swipe a message to someone.

It took me several moments before I realized that Corey had given me a prime opportunity to question Sailor's dad, and I mentally recanted what I'd thought about Corey not being as handsome.

I quietly cleared my throat to capture Ian's attention. "I know you. I've seen your picture at the Expanding Universe. You're Karyn's ex-husband, Ian Strickland."

He slid a sideways glance at me, a touch of interest showing in his hazel eyes. "I am."

I gave him a consolatory smile. "I'm sorry for your loss."

Ian lifted a shoulder and let it drop. "It's not my loss. Whatever feelings I had for her died years ago."

I nodded in understanding. "But it still affects you since your daughter is hurt by what happened."

He lifted his chin in answer. "True enough."

Ian turned back to his phone. He didn't seem inclined to talk much, but I needed to capitalize on the moment. I dropped my shoulders to appear relaxed and tried again. "You know, I talked to Sailor only a few days ago. She really wants to stay in that house."

He huffed and looked at me again. "She doesn't always get what she wants."

I gave him a knowing nod. "Teenagers. I heard her talking to the police not long ago. She said she took the money for tuition."

He widened his eyes in shock. "Is that why I'm here? She's been arrested for stealing?"

Apparently, no one had informed him of anything other than that they had Sailor detained. I lifted a hand to calm him. "It was just money out of her mother's office. She didn't rob anyone, except maybe you."

He clenched his jaw and shook his head. "I know this is all very upsetting to her, and she doesn't like me telling her when she'll get her money. But her tuition is paid, as is the mortgage on her mother's house. She has enough for food and basic expenses. If she wants more for other things, she just needs to ask, and I'll consider it."

I sent him a look of sympathy, grateful that I didn't have teenagers of my own to fight with. "I'm sorry. It's certainly not an easy time for any of you."

He snorted. "You can say that again."

Then he stood. "I need to speak with my lawyer, find out what the hold up is. No one has told me any of this, and that's unacceptable. She's still a minor for God's sake."

He exited the room, leaving the door wide open.

I wondered how long it would take before someone chased him down. Although, it might result in him getting the answers he wanted and deserved.

After waiting another ten minutes for Corey to return, I decided to make a break for it myself. If he wanted to know what I'd learned, which wasn't much, then he could track me down later.

TWENTY

When Sailor walked into Meowkins the following morning, I had to admit I was shocked. I had a line of customers waiting for coffee, so she shot me a snarky look and headed inside the Purry Parlor.

I turned and touched Aeri on the shoulder. "I'm going to send Nicole out to help you. Sailor Strickland just walked into the parlor."

Aeri widened her eyes in surprise. "Yeah. You go. I wonder what she has to say."

I snorted. "If the snarky expression on her face was any indication, she has a few unpleasant things planned."

Aeri moved to the counter and helped the next customer in line.

Inside the Purry Parlor, I found Nicole and Sailor sitting on the couch, chatting. Sailor had Friskers on her lap once again, and the smile on her face disappeared when she saw me.

I turned my gaze to Nicole. "Do you mind helping Aeri for a few minutes? We're kind of slammed out there."

She glanced between me and Sailor and then stood. "Of course not."

Oliver, who was a faded version of Friskers with his sand-colored fur, trotted toward me, and I scooped him up for emotional support. I sat in the spot that Nicole had vacated and prepared myself for verbal abuse. "You obviously have something that you want to say to me."

The anger in her eyes quickly morphed to pain. "Why did you have to do that last night? Why couldn't you mind your own business?"

I shrugged. "I'm sure I don't need to tell you, but someone murdered your mother, Sailor. I know you don't want to hear it, but that person is likely someone who was very close to her."

Her chin quivered, and she swiped at the tears on her cheeks. "And you think it's me. You think that me breaking into the studio last night has something to do with it."

I shrugged. "It's the second crime that's been committed there in a short number of days. You told the police that the money was for tuition, but your dad said that's already been paid."

She shook her head repeatedly. "You are so clueless."

I let the barb of her words ping off me. "Then enlighten me."

She turned, looking me directly in the eye, and I could see that her anger had returned. "The money was for Alisha. For *her* tuition. She's so smart and the best friend I've ever had, and you might have killed her chances for a brilliant future."

The air in my lungs fizzled like it would from a balloon. That was certainly not the answer I'd expected. The knowledge was a hard lump to swallow. "Then I'm sorry for that. I would never want to do anything to harm Alisha."

"Too late for that now." She covered her mouth as more tears came. "How am I supposed to tell her and her mom? I tried to talk to Alisha this morning about what had happened last night, and I couldn't. I just couldn't. My mom's death has already been so hard on them, and now this?"

Her heartbreak slayed me, and I was grateful that Friskers was there to give her comfort.

I searched for something I could do to fix things. "Has Alisha applied for financial aid? She might be eligible to have a good portion of her costs paid."

Sailor shrugged. "I don't know. Her mom said that if I could get the money, it would only be a loan, that she'd pay me back."

I remembered that Bobbi had been named in Karyn's will. "Once the funds from your mom's estate are released, right?"

She nodded.

I placed a hand on her arm. "It's going to be okay, Sailor. Alisha will be able to go to school. If worse came to worst, she could get a short-term school loan. If she's as bright as you say she is, this won't stop her."

Sailor glanced at me with watery but hopeful eyes. "Are you sure?"

"I'm sure. Tell her to talk to the financial aid office. They can help her with everything."

She studied me a moment longer and then exhaled a shaky breath. She dropped her gaze to Friskers. "I know that I shouldn't have broken in last night. But the deadline is today. Bobbi had some money saved. I hope it was enough to secure Alisha's spot and that she can pay the rest later."

In that moment, I was grateful for all the lessons life had taught me, especially the realization that despite hardships, ultimately things would work out one way or the other. Life would go on, and there was so much more to the universe than my small world. "It'll be okay. Even if Alisha had to wait until next semester to attend school, she'll be fine."

Sailor shook her head. "But we want to go together."

"I know, and maybe you'll still be able to. Try talking to your dad."

She rolled her eyes. "He won't help." Then she growled in frustration. "If Bobbi would have remembered to give me her key. If I would have remembered to grab it, none of this would have happened. But I was there, and I needed to get that money."

I lifted my brow. "Bobbi knew you were going there last night?"

Sailor nodded. "She'd asked to borrow money from me now that my mom isn't around. When I told her that I didn't have enough, she told me about the white envelope in my mom's filing cabinet."

"Why did you go at night? Why not while the studio was open?"

She shrugged. "Bobbi said it would be better if no one saw so that no one could tell my dad. That way he couldn't stop me. When I realized I didn't have the key, I decided that it might not be a bad idea if it looked like a robbery. Then Bobbi wouldn't have to worry about paying me back. No one was using that money anyway, and it was only a little broken window."

I frowned. "Did Bobbi often ask your mom for money?"

She shrugged. "Sometimes, though my mom had been kind of prickly about it lately. She even stopped paying for Alisha to go to private school with me for a month. But then Alisha said she started again. I was really glad that she did because I was about to tell my mom that if Alisha couldn't go then I wouldn't either."

"That's a strong bond of friendship."

Sailor managed a smile. "Alisha means everything to me."

I patted her on the arm. "I'm sorry for the trouble I've caused you both. I was only trying to help."

She accepted my apology with a nod. "I'm sorry, too. I shouldn't have done what I did."

"We live and learn and then do better next time."

She gazed down at Friskers. "Yeah."

I stood. "I should get back to work. Walk you out?"

She hugged Friskers tighter to her. "Is it okay if I stay awhile? I really like it here. It feels safe."

I smiled and nodded. "You go right ahead."

TWENTY-ONE

For the rest of the workday, I mulled over what Sailor had said to me, and one thing didn't make sense. Why didn't Bobbi just take the money herself once Sailor had agreed to it? Why make Sailor go into the office at all?

Yeah, Sailor didn't want someone to catch her and tell her dad what she'd done, which was exactly what had happened, ironically. But surely Bobbi would have had many opportunities to be there alone. And no one would question her if they'd caught her in Karyn's office. Was it just the appearance of taking money that she'd been adverse to?

Aeri had left for the day, and I was wiping down tables, when Nicole emerged from the Purry Parlor. "The kitties are all fed and good for the night," she said.

I straightened. "Are you free tonight? I thought maybe I'd drop in for another yoga class."

Her gaze turned puzzled. "You said you didn't want to go until next week. You wanted a couple of days of rest, and the coven's Midsummer bonfire is tomorrow night."

"I changed my mind about both. I'm skipping the ritual this time. After what Vivian and Jocelyn did, I need some time away from them. Plus, I don't need everyone gawking at me and whispering because they all know I'm living with a demon."

She nodded in understanding. "Yeah, I get that. So why yoga?"

"I have some questions for Bobbi, so I thought I'd go early under the pretense of waiting for yoga to start."

Her eyes brightened. "More sleuthing? I like it. Sure, I'm up for a class."

I grinned. "Awesome. I'll meet you there."

After locking up, I hurried home to get my workout clothes and hoped to run everything past Gideon. He usually had great insight and helped me see things more clearly. Unfortunately, he wasn't home. Again.

So, I fed my kitties, jumped in my car, and headed back down the mountain toward the Expanding Universe. Though the class wouldn't start for another thirty minutes, four cars were already in the lot. One was Bobbi's, and the other was Justin's yellow Jeep, which made me think that the universe had presented me with another opportunity to talk to him, too. There were enough people in the building that I wasn't afraid to approach him this time.

I headed toward the weight-lifting room first. When I stepped inside, I was surprised to find that it looked vastly different than the weight rooms I'd seen on TV. It did have the same weights and machines, but lovely Zen music played in the background. Several potted trees had been placed around the room, and beautiful pieces of framed art with inspiring quotes were interspersed between full length mirrors.

I spotted Justin immediately, and of course, he was wearing another black tank top. I had to admit he was attractive with his dark hair and square jawline, but he wasn't worth betraying a friend.

Unfortunately, he was busy coaching another client. He caught sight of me standing in the doorway and gestured at me with a jut of his chin. "Looking to schedule some time with me?"

Feeling utterly awkward, I smiled and took a step back. "Uh, yeah, maybe. I wanted to talk to you, but I'll come back later."

I didn't wait for a response before I turned and strode away.

I scanned rooms on my way back toward the reception area and peeked into the darkened workout studio, looking for Bobbi, but there was no sign of her. In the locker room, I paused to change clothes so that I looked legit and then headed down the other hall where Karyn's office was located.

And that's exactly where I found Bobbi. Sitting in Karyn's chair, typing on her keyboard. She yelped when she spotted me. "Oh, my goodness, Daisy. You startled me."

Something unsettling swirled in the air, and I gave her a cautious smile. "Sorry."

She quickly stood and took several steps toward me. "Is there something I can help you with?"

I tilted my head, wanting to ask her the same thing. "I had some questions about the incident with Sailor."

She widened her eyes and curved her lips into a worried smile, all which seemed a little over the top. "Sailor? Did something happen to her?"

"You know. The break-in that happened a couple of nights ago."

This time, she had a look of genuine concern on her face. "Someone broke into Sailor's house?"

I narrowed my gaze in confusion and stepped closer to the desk. "No, she broke in here, to get money out of this office."

All color drained from Bobbi's face. "Why...why would she do that?"

I glanced at the open file folder on the desk and saw what looked to be a list of passwords.

Bobbi twisted and flipped the cover of the file shut. "That's private information."

The fearful look in her eyes stunned me. The woman had always seemed so sincere, so caring about her daughter, about Karyn. She'd even passed out when I'd told her of Karyn's death.

But had that truly been because Karyn had been murdered, or was it because Bobbi was already in a compromised state because she'd just taken a life?

I glanced toward the computer screen, and panic replaced the fear in Bobbi's eyes. She leaned toward the computer as if to turn it off or otherwise prevent me from viewing what she'd been doing.

The spell I'd used on Sailor only days earlier flew from my mouth, and Bobbi landed hard on the white leather chair. She scrambled to get up, and I cast it again. "Stay where you are."

I moved closer to where I could properly view the screen. As I did, I sensed Bobbi's urgency to flee increased exponentially.

A quick peek at the computer confirmed my suspicions when I recognized the logo of the Sweet Mountain Meadows First National Bank.

Bobbi shoved me hard, knocking me backward in her attempt to get away. I slammed her with another spell, and she fell flat on her belly, landing halfway between the office and the hall.

I hurried forward, straddled her back, and pinned her with my body weight. She flailed her arms trying to reach me and bent her knees trying to kick me. Unfortunately for her, I was stronger.

She almost bucked me off when I reached into my bag for my phone, but I managed to dial Corey's number with one tap on my screen. I tapped the button that would put the call on speaker and dropped the phone to the carpet so that I could use both hands to hold Bobbi.

"Hey, Daisy," he said. "What's up?"

"I have your perpetrator," I said, sounding breathless.

Bobbi let out a growl that echoed through the office.

"What the? Where are you?" he asked.

Bobbi made a more powerful attempt to disengage herself, and it took me a moment to wrangle her in before I answered Corey. "Karyn's office. Hurry. It's Bobbi."

"Coming."

He didn't say anything else, but I could hear shuffling noises, and I hoped he was still there. Then he barked at someone, telling them to radio Officer Kemp to meet him at the Expanding Universe.

"Corey?"

"Yeah?" He sounded a bit breathless himself. "Tell me what you can. Are you in danger? Do you have eyes on her?"

Bobbi made another forceful attempt, and it wasn't until I saw my phone go sailing into the hall that I realized she'd grabbed it. It landed with a loud thud somewhere beyond my sight.

I yanked her arm back and pinned it beneath my knee. "Corey?" I called out to see if I could still hear him and received nothing but silence.

It was my turn to growl. "You better not have broken my phone."

She fought against me for several minutes until she must have found a burst of superhuman strength because she managed to knock me off balance. She scrambled into the hall on hands and knees, while I righted myself and got to my feet.

I hurried into the hall to find Bobbi frozen only a few feet away, and Corey striding toward her.

Bobbi pivoted toward me, and Corey whipped the gun from his holster. "Stop right there, Bobbi. You have nowhere left to run."

I saw the look in her eye, gauging whether she could get past me, so I lifted my hand, too. I didn't have a gun, and I likely looked ridiculous to Corey and Officer Kemp, but she knew I had the power to knock her down.

She stayed staring at me with blazing hatred.

I sent her a disappointed look. "Why did you do it, Bobbi? For the money? For tuition like Sailor said?"

She shook her head at me, looking as though I'd never understand. "Alisha deserves every bit as much as Sailor. More, in fact. She's bright, far more intelligent than me, Sailor, or her mom."

"So, you killed Karyn in order to get your inheritance now?"

Corey reached her and pulled both hands behind her back to cuff her. He read her rights to her, but she barely seemed to notice.

Instead, she scoffed at me. "No. Karyn was worth more to me alive than dead."

I nodded slowly as the pieces fit together. "Because you had access to her bank accounts."

Bobbi shook her head in disgust. "She had so much money and never kept track of it. What I took didn't hurt her."

"But she caught you, didn't she? Like I just did, logged into her account."

She turned her face away from me and didn't respond.

I met Corey's gaze, and he nodded. Then he focused on Kemp. "Take her to the station. I'll be right behind you."

Corey waited until they had disappeared from the hall before he turned back to me. "You okay?" he asked softly.

I huffed, still trying to tame the heat in my veins. "Tussling with her wasn't exactly the workout I was looking for when I came here."

He chuckled. "I was worried when our call got disconnected."

I searched the floor for my phone and spotted it just behind him. "She threw my phone down the hall. I hope she didn't break it."

He bent, picked it up, and examined it before he held it out to me. "Screen's not broken."

"That's good." I pushed the button to unlock it, and the screen lit up like normal. "Seems okay. She must have somehow ended the call when she tossed it."

He nodded. "I'm going to need a statement."

I sighed in resignation. "Giving statements is my least favorite part of this."

"Worse than hand-to-hand combat?"

I chuckled then. "No. Can I at least go to my yoga class first? I feel like I'd give a much better statement if my mind is centered."

It was an excuse, but I felt like it was a good one.

He smiled. "Sure. It'll take us a while to question her anyway."

I thanked him, and he turned to leave. Then he paused and glanced back at me, giving me a quick once-over. "Nice workout gear."

Before I could form a response, he winked and strode down the hall.

I dropped my face into my hands and shook my head. I really did need that yoga class.

EPILOGUE

Midsummer arrived, the day as sunny and beautiful as it should be. Gideon was still sound asleep when I rose early in the morning, and I tried to be as quiet as possible so that I wouldn't disturb him.

I wasn't sure what time he'd come home, but the last time I'd woken and checked, it had been after three in the morning, and he hadn't returned yet. He had to be exhausted.

I made breakfast, brewed a pot of sun celebration tea, and dressed in clothes suitable for working in my garden. After filling a travel mug with the tea, I grabbed my journal and favorite pen and headed for the back door.

Freya met me there, meowing her intention to join me, so I let her tag along. She happily trotted as we followed the trail to the clearing where Gideon had created my secret garden.

When I arrived, I was stunned. Sun showered down on flowers and herbs that had been planted only a few days ago. They thrived and bloomed, looking as though they'd been in the ground for a month or more. "Freya," I said on an exhale. "Will you look at this?"

At some point, Gideon had done more work in the area besides just the magical growth. Two comfortable garden chairs and a small green bistro table sat to one side, with a fire pit dug into the ground nearby.

I placed my hand over my heart and blinked back tears of joy. "I can't believe it."

After I stared in awe for several moments, Freya asked me to sit. It wasn't until I turned to where she sat in one of the chairs that I realized I hadn't interpreted her meow or read her body language.

I'd actually heard the words clearly in my head.

I widened my eyes and stared at her. "I heard that, Freya. Heard you."

My beautiful gray familiar stood, turned in a circle, and then sat again, looking very pleased. I hurried over and fell into the chair next to her. She jumped on my lap and stared into my eyes.

I petted her as she purred. "Say something else."

Love you.

I gasped my amazement. "How is this even happening? How did you learn? I've been meaning to practice with you, but you did this all on your own."

She rubbed her face against my hand, and the answer came swiftly and surely. Gideon.

I didn't know if it was a magic spell that he'd cast over the garden that allowed us to communicate better or if he'd worked with her. But whichever it was, I couldn't be happier.

Freya sat on my lap as I sipped the white tea that had been fused with lemon, orange, and just the slightest hint of ginger. Birds sang in the trees while butterflies flitted from flower to flower.

When I pulled out my journal, she jumped to the ground and headed off to inspect the garden. I wrote for a while and then dozed in the dappled sun.

I wasn't sure how long I'd languished in my comfortable chair when my heart woke me. I opened my eyes to see Gideon strolling along the path with a blanket in one hand and a basket in the other.

Our gazes connected, and he grinned. "Looks like you were enjoying a bit of a nap."

I stretched and stood. "Maybe."

He reached me, set the basket on the table, and tossed the blanket over one chair. Then he pulled me into his arms. "Naps are a decadent pleasure that should be enjoyed whenever possible."

I laughed. "I might say the same about you."

Black flashed around the edges of his irises even as his eyes lit up. "I definitely like the sound of that."

"Oh, my Goddess, Freya? Did you teach her how to talk to me?"

He shrugged. "I might have given her a hint or two, but the work was all hers."

"It's just incredible. And the garden is, too. Thank you so much."

He held me tighter and studied my eyes. "Nothing but a bit of magic."

I disagreed with a shake of my head. "It's more than magic. It's beauty. It's...love."

"That it is."

I gave him a long, slow kiss that melted me all the way to my toes before I pulled away and glanced at the basket. "What did you bring?"

He smiled. "Some lunch. I thought we could hang out here for a while, enjoying the pleasures around us. Then when we're hungry again, I'll cook dinner, and we can return here afterward to light a fire for Midsummer."

Again, I was surprised that he knew witch customs so well. "That sounds absolutely perfect."

As we unpacked the basket, he nudged me. "Congratulations on solving the case."

I snorted. "It was a little tougher than the others. I still find it hard to believe Bobbi could have killed her friend."

He arched his brow. "It sounds to me as if she's not all there mentally. I'm sure they'll test her before they prosecute."

I sighed. "I'm glad I'm not the one who has to decide such things. I'm also relieved that I didn't have to break the news to Alisha. Those poor girls have been through so much."

"They have each other, though, don't they?"

I nodded and then narrowed my gaze at him. "How is it you know so much about the case? And that I helped solve it?"

He chuckled. "I have my ways."

I frowned. "Speaking of that, why didn't you show up last night while I was restraining Bobbi? Didn't that situation trigger something for you?"

He glanced back to the basket and pulled out two bottles of spring water. "I did check on you."

I placed my hand on his arm. "It's okay. I'm not mad or anything. It just surprises me."

Another moment passed before he looked at me again. "I sensed that you were in a difficult situation, but you were never frightened."

I shook my head. "No, I think I felt empowered. I did have to use my magic a couple of times."

His gaze grew serious. "As you should when you're in a difficult situation. It's a gift that you're lucky to have available to you at all times."

That it was. "I should show more gratitude for it and give it more attention. There is a reason they call it *practicing* witchcraft after all."

"Yes. I wholeheartedly support you in that regard."

Something in the way he spoke sounded off. "Is there a reason that you're so encouraging?"

He gave a firm shake of his head. "Nothing more than usual."

He glanced around. "With the firepit and water in the nearby pond, the rich earth below us and a breeze in the trees, I would think this might be an excellent place to hone your skills."

I studied him for a moment. When he smiled at me, with his eyes full of love and light, I decided I must have misjudged his tone.

I'd spent too much time worrying lately. And I'd lived long enough to know that doing so would crowd out wonderful moments like the one right in front of me.

With that thought, I let the beauty of the midsummer day fill me, and I wrapped my arms around Gideon's shoulders, wanting to share my happiness with him. "I think you might be right. I can't wait to get started practicing, but for today, I just want to enjoy my time here with you."

He grinned and pulled me into his arms. "Then let's get started."

Midlife in the Fast Lane, Sweet Mountain Witches, Book Four, is coming in January 2022.

Keep reading for an excerpt from Murder and Moonstones, Book One of the Crystal Cove series, where Gideon makes his first appearance in Book Three. If you've already enjoyed those books, check out the Teas and Temptations Mysteries. I think you'll like them.

****

Dear Reader:

Thanks for joining me on the journey inside Daisy's world. I hope you enjoyed the story. If you did, please consider leaving a review. It's simple, and it helps me in a profound way to continue to bring you stories you enjoy. All you need to do is:

Return to the purchasing page.

Scroll down to the Customer Review Section.

Look for Review This Product

Click on Write A Customer Review

Your review helps me tremendously, and it can be as simple as a short and sweet, "I liked it".

Also, make sure to sign up for my newsletter and follow me on Amazon for release news of future books and for special offers.

Newsletter signup: www.CindyStark.com
Amazon: https://www.amazon.com/Cindy-Stark/e/B008FT394W

Thank you, very much, and happy reading,
Cindy

Excerpt from Murder and Moonstones
Crystal Cove Mysteries
Book One

Opal Mayland was close. So close.

Less than twenty minutes stood between her and Crystal Cove, Oregon, her childhood home. She'd spent the last six years in Sedona, Arizona, learning her craft at the center of a powerful vortex.

She appreciated the teachers who'd worked with her on spells and potions, since that opportunity didn't exist for her in Crystal Cove, but she'd had enough of the desert heat. The lush green forests full of alders, spruce, and fir trees had called to her soul, and now she was finally back to the Oregon coast.

This morning, she'd woken super early so she could roll into town just past noon. Now, she was so close to home that she could taste the salt on the late springtime air that blew in through the car window.

Opal pressed harder on the accelerator, and the needle on the speedometer crept up. Her sparkly blue Mustang growled as its engine kicked in, and it eased into the next curve as smooth as the surface of a mountain lake.

She smiled, loving the thrill.

Rain speckled the windshield, and she turned on the wipers to whisk it away. She didn't mind. She loved the rain and salty ocean breezes more than just about anything in the world. She'd missed the Pacific Northwest's beauty almost as much as she'd missed her grandfather.

The urge to throw her arms around her grandpa, the town's police chief, was strong, and she hoped he wouldn't lecture her for coming home unannounced. She also hoped he'd learned to keep his share of crazy in check when it came to any kind of paranormal persons other than her. The fact that he'd accidentally married a witch never failed to give Opal a laugh.

The sight of a dark blue police SUV nestled amongst a cluster of trees along the side of the road reined in her thoughts. She flicked her gaze to the speedometer and cringed. Fourteen over the posted limit.

Red and blue lights flashed to life, and she groaned. She didn't need her grandfather to hear that the first thing she'd done on her first day back was to get a speeding ticket. He'd never let her live it down.

She let off the gas and weighed her chances of being able to talk the officer out of giving her a citation. She'd guess fifty-fifty, which wasn't great. But then another option popped into her mind.

What if she tried a redirection spell?

She'd been dying to try it out in the real world, but did she dare? If it worked, it would cause the officer to switch his focus to something else. If it didn't, then she might end up with a citation. So, really, what did she have to lose?

The loud chirp of the officer's siren brought her thoughts to the present and warned she was out of time.

She had to cast the spell now or never.

Do it, her inner voice said. *Do it.*

She glanced in the rearview mirror and released a steadying breath. "See that tree? See that ground? Stop your car and turn around. What you need is not me. Turn away, so mote it be."

The little buzz that she received from casting a successful spell heated her blood. Her mentors had warned not to use magic for selfish reasons too often, lest she invoke Karma to balance her efforts, but this one little thing shouldn't hurt.

She smiled and pressed the accelerator, expecting the officer would pull to the side of the road and then head in the opposite direction.

Seconds passed, and her nerves began to twitch. She continually flicked her gaze between the road ahead and her rearview mirror, but the officer wasn't stopping. In fact, he seemed closer than ever. The SUV's emergency lights remained bright, even with the increased spray of water her tires kicked up. Uncertainty tightened her throat, and she swallowed.

She'd try it again. Maybe she hadn't said something quite right.

"See that tree?" she whispered harsh and fast. "See that ground? Stop your car and turn around. What you need is not me. Turn away, so mote it be."

The officer turned on the siren full blast. It startled her so much that she thought her heart might stop beating.

Sweet mother of pearl.

Her spell hadn't worked, and now the officer was in hot pursuit after *her*. She'd become one of those idiot people her grandfather had told her about, the ones who thought they could somehow evade the law. She needed to pull over before the officer called for backup.

Her pulse thundered in her ears as she signaled, slowed, and came to a stop at the side of the road. The chance of talking her way out of a citation now had dropped significantly.

Then again, maybe she didn't need to worry so much. After all, she was home. As long as her grandfather hadn't switched out the entire police force, chances were good that she'd know the officer. Maybe she could plead for mercy and end up with only a strong lecture about speeding. This was manageable. Not the end of the world.

She exhaled and reined in her fears.

Spatters of rain on the windshield and the side mirror kept her from immediately identifying the tall, obviously male officer who approached. She lowered her window and cast her gaze downward in contrition, prepared to apologize.

"Step out of your car, ma'am."

The fierce authority in his voice surprised her, and she swung her gaze over her shoulder to see him better. The dark-haired officer with gorgeous green eyes placed his hand in warning on the butt of his gun.

Surprised, her breath caught in her throat, and she choked. "No, wait. You don't—"

"I *said*, step out of the car."

His voice was even and clear, and she had no doubt he meant what he said. Her brain emptied of all thoughts, and her hands flew into the air as though they had a mind of their own. The officer opened her door, and she awkwardly swiveled on her seat and stepped out into the light, misty rain.

The officer, perhaps a few years older than her, wore an official Crystal Cove Police Department jacket embroidered with his last name, Keller. Short, midnight hair peeked from beneath his plastic-covered hat. But those intense green eyes intimidated her the most.

Officer Keller glanced beyond her and into the car as though searching for signs that she might be dangerous. "Name?"

She swallowed. "Opal Mayland."

His gaze pierced hers again. "Do you have a driver's license, Ms. Mayland?"

She nodded. "It's in the car. Should I get it?"

"Not until I tell you to."

He scrutinized every inch of her, leaving her feeling vulnerable and exposed. "Are you carrying any weapons, Ms. Mayland?"

Her negative response sounded more like a squeak.

He narrowed his eyes. "Why didn't you stop when I first flashed my lights?"

Oh dear. She widened her eyes into innocent ovals. "I did stop. That's why we're standing here in the rain."

Irritation sparked in his eyes, and she swore they darkened. He obviously did not appreciate her flippant response. "You did *eventually*. From my perspective, it appeared as though you'd attempted to outrun me first."

Her heart thundered in her chest, and she shook her head quickly. "No, sir. I...I panicked."

The white lie fell easily from her lips.

He lifted his brow, indicating he expected more from her in the way of an excuse.

She exhaled a nervous breath. "I know I should have stopped right away, but this crazy thought entered my mind, telling me I needed to hurry and get to a pull-off before I moved out of your way. So, I went faster. Then I realized that you were actually pulling *me* over, not chasing after someone else."

Even to her own ears, her lie sounded utterly ridiculous. She could only imagine what he must be thinking.

He stared, stone-faced. "You expect me to believe that."

Praying that he would do exactly that, she opened her hands, palms up and shrugged. "I have anxieties and don't always react in the most appropriate way."

She watched his face carefully, working hard to keep hers a mask of virtue. Instinctively, she reached out with her senses, trying to discover his hidden emotions but came back with nothing. Perhaps she should tell him who her grandfather was so that she could generate credibility, but her heart warned against it.

He blinked and glanced inside her car again. "I'll take your license and registration now."

"Yes, sir." She snatched her purse from the passenger seat to retrieve her license and then leaned over to grab the registration from the glovebox, all under his watchful eyes. She stood and held out her documents, hoping her friendly smile would ease the tension.

He showed no emotional reaction to her gesture and turned his attention to her driver's license. Then he flicked his gaze back to her. "Opal Mayland from Sedona, Arizona."

She tried a smile once more. "Yes."

He glanced between the license and her face, and then gave a curt nod. "Wait here, please."

With an unhurried swagger, he returned to his vehicle. She sagged against her damp car, and let the rain soothe her stress. Water was the least of her problems. She didn't need magic to know that things with Officer Keller hadn't gone well.

She could already hear a repeat of her grandfather's overused lecture on not driving as though the devil chased her. The thought of it tangled her nerves tighter. She was too old for him to take away her keys, but the disappointment in his eyes would be worse.

The sound of a car door closing drew her attention. Officer Keller sauntered back to her in an annoyingly confident manner. "Here you go, Ms. Mayland. Your record appears clean, with no outstanding warrants."

She could thank the stars for that. "Can I go, then?"

He chuckled. "Do you know how fast you were driving when I clocked you?"

Apparently, he'd accepted her explanation for not stopping, but she wasn't off the hook yet.

She considered his question. If she admitted she was speeding, he'd likely ticket her. Her only option was to continue to play innocent. "Uh...no. I didn't think I was going too fast."

He cleared his throat. "I clocked you at fourteen miles over the speed limit, and that was before you...panicked."

She sighed. "I'm sorry, officer, I didn't mean to speed. I've been driving for days, and I'm so ready to be out of the car. I was focused on my destination and didn't realize how fast I was going until I saw your lights."

Which was mostly true. She *did* like to drive fast, but she *had* been distracted.

He seemed interested in her response. "Are you visiting the area, then?"

Not exactly visiting, but she couldn't say she was a native to Crystal Cove without him asking questions about her family. With it being a small town, eventually he'd learn she was the chief's granddaughter, but hopefully, by then, the incident would have blown over.

"I'm headed to Crystal Cove."

He nodded in appreciation. "It's a beautiful town."

She answered with a smile. "I do love the ocean."

He relaxed his shoulders, giving her hope. "I'm going to do you a favor since you're visiting from Arizona. We wouldn't want you to get the wrong idea about the friendliness of Oregonians."

Thank the stars. He was going to let her off with a warning.

Instead, he held out a clipboard, and her short-lived happiness plummeted. "I've written the ticket for only nine miles over the limit, which should help your pocketbook considerably."

She swallowed her initial sarcastic response about him being too kind and swiped the clipboard from him.

He didn't seem to notice her small display of irritation. "Your signature is not an admittance of guilt. It only notes that you've received the citation. You have the option of appearing in court, or if you prefer to pay for your citation without contesting it, visit the website listed at the bottom."

She signed the paper with an annoyed flourish and shoved the clipboard toward him.

He tore off a copy of the ticket and handed it to her. "Take care out there, Ms. Mayland. Moisture on the roadways can make them slicker than normal."

So, she'd been told. "Yes, sir, Officer Keller."

He'd started to turn but paused when she used his name. He narrowed his eyes and then glanced at the name on his uniform and nodded. "Have a good day."

After he turned away, she rolled her eyes. Cops weren't the only ones who noticed details.

She climbed into her car, her clothes now damp enough to notice, and she sighed. This day was not turning out like she'd hoped at all. Her only wish was that he'd keep silent about the citation or not deem it worthy of conversation. After all, it was only one ticket out of plenty that he'd written.

****

Opal drove exactly the posted speed limit as she passed Crystal Cove's city limit sign and waited for the sense of home to surround her like a warm hug. When it came, her eyes welled with tears. She'd been gone too long and had forgotten exactly how much this town meant to her.

Except for her time in Sedona, she'd lived in the small oceanside village her whole life. Her mother and grandmother were buried in the cemetery at the top of the hill. She'd spent years running the halls of the old Victorian cottage her grandfather owned and countless hours reclaiming her mother's garden. Her best friend, Penelope, who'd been the only one to visit her in Sedona, still lived in the small house overlooking the ocean that had been in Penelope's family for years.

Of course, there were certain unfortunate things about her past years in Crystal Cove that she could never forget, either. Like how she'd walked the beach for days after her old boyfriend had crushed her heart, and how that had led to her asking to attend witch school out of state. Despite the fact that her grandfather had hunted paranormal beings and wasn't keen on any of them living in his town, he'd given his blessing. They'd both shed tears the day she'd left.

She'd grown during her time away, but she'd missed her friends and family. Not to mention the level of pure energy the town received from being sandwiched between the forests and the Pacific Ocean. Energy that could cleanse her spirit of the negativity that she'd received from her unfortunate encounter with that officer. Energy that would give her a sense of renewal and help her to restart her day in a positive way.

She fingered the moonstone pendant that had once been her mother's. It always reminded her that as long as her heart continued to beat, she could start over. And there was no time like the present.

Instead of heading directly to the police station, where she'd likely find her grandfather, she turned on the first street at the edge of town, which led toward the ocean. She'd already intended to complete a small, personal ritual that night in her mother's garden, one that would mark the end of one leg of her journey. Then she could start the next with renewed hope and energy. But why wait?

Her car bumped along the uneven road that paralleled the fresh-water river winding its way to the salty ocean. When she spotted a grassy area, easy to reach from the street, she slowed and stopped alongside the Chemawa River.

She'd learned the power of a renewing ritual from her witch sisters not long after she'd arrived in Sedona. It had helped her to calm her fears about leaving her grandfather alone and helped to bury thoughts of her old boyfriend deep beneath the surface of her memories, where they wouldn't see the light of day.

The ritual was much like a meditation, but one where she invoked the power of the elements to help her. She tore a page from the small notebook she kept in her glovebox and wrote down her intentions and desires, which would focus her energy. Then she folded the paper into her palm and exited the car.

Delightful, addictive power accompanied the breeze rolling in from the ocean. It caressed her skin like a lover's kiss. She paused for a moment to soak it in and let the unseen energy soothe her soul. *This*. This was what she'd missed the most.

Many considered Crystal Cove nothing more than a small, seaside town, but she recognized the forces surging through the air. Strong, beautiful energy, freshly-cleansed by rain. Her grandfather always sensed it, too, but he preferred to think the magic belonged only to the ocean. At least he didn't deny that it was there.

She shut her car door and glanced about to see who else might be in the area. She wanted to focus on her emotions and connecting to nature without being disturbed. A maroon sedan sat parked on the opposite side, but thankfully, no one was around.

She opened the trunk, slid a small black case toward her, and extracted a fireproof ceramic bowl that she'd purchased in a pottery shop in Sedona. The gorgeous piece boasted swirls of red and burgundy and gave her a thrill every time she used it. With as wet as it was in Crystal Cove, it was unlikely she'd catch the grass on fire, but she liked to be careful.

Opal made her way toward the river. She created a path through the ankle-high grasses, down a gentle slope toward the river, and then walked until her senses told her she'd found the perfect spot.

Water flowed past in a lazy fashion, unaware of the cleansing turbulence that waited for it once it reached the vast ocean. She chose an open area amongst the twinberry and ninebark where she could see the river and sank to her knees before falling back on her bottom.

Moisture soaked through her jeans, but she didn't pay it much notice. She was already damp, and one couldn't live in a coastal town in Oregon and expect to stay dry.

She curled her legs to the side of her, placed the ceramic bowl in the grass, and closed her eyes. The sound of passing water calmed her senses. Deep breaths cleared any stress she'd carried from the long drive and allowed her to focus her thoughts.

When she was ready, she placed the paper with her written intentions inside the bowl. With a few whispered words, one corner of the paper caught fire. She cupped her hand along the side of the bowl to protect the swaying flame.

The tender flame grew as it consumed paper, and she held a hand out, allowing the heat to tickle her fingers. "I call to the element of Fire," she whispered.

The fire jumped, died low, and then jumped again, It circled the paper and turned it black as it released her hopes and desires into the universe.

When nothing was left but ashes, she pulled grass from the earth and lifted a pinch of soil. She rubbed the moist dirt between her thumb and forefinger and allowed it to fall into the bowl. "I call to the element of Earth."

She wasn't finished, but already, her soul felt lighter.

She exhaled the remnants of stress and stood, making her way to the edge of the riverbank. She poured the ashes and dirt into one hand and tossed them into the breeze. Some sank to the ground beneath her, while others caught the wind and drifted away into the water. "I call to the element of Air."

Carefully, she bent and scooped cool water into the bowl to wash away any remaining ashes, swirling her fingers around the edge before dumping it out. "I call to the element of Water."

She stood. "Great Goddess, hear my plea. Take negative energy away from me. Transform it into light and love. Grant these things from up above. This I ask, so mote it be."

A sense of calm filled her as she lifted her gaze to the sky. She was home and could be at peace now. The Goddess provided many beautiful things for her to enjoy and be thankful for. The fresh air. The gently flowing river, and—

The sight of something large bobbing in the water startled her, and she inhaled a quick breath. She fully expected to see a log or other debris, but that wasn't what was there at all.

Fear gripped her, and she took several clumsy steps backward. "A body," she said, barely able to breathe. "There's a body in the water."

Murder and Moonstones
Book One, Crystal Cove Mysteries
is available at Amazon.com

BOOK LIST

SWEET MOUNTAIN WITCHES (PG–Rated Fun):
Midlife or Death
For Once in My Midlife
One Midlife to Live
Midlife in the Fast Lane

CRYSTAL COVE COZY MYSTERIES (PG–Rated Fun):
Murder and Moonstones
Brews and Bloodstone
Curses and Carnelian
Killer Kyanite
Rumors and Rose Quartz
Hexes and Hematite

TEAS & TEMPTATIONS COZY MYSTERIES (PG–Rated Fun):
Once Wicked
Twice Hexed
Three Times Charmed
Four Warned
The Fifth Curse
It's All Sixes
Spellbound Seven
Elemental Eight
Nefarious Nine
Hijacked Honeymoon
A Witch Without a Spell

BLACKWATER CANYON RANCH (Western Sexy Romance):
Caleb
Oliver
Justin

Piper

Jesse

ASPEN SERIES (Small Town Sexy Romance):

Wounded (Prequel)

Relentless

Lawless

Cowboys and Angels

Come Back To Me

Surrender

Reckless

Tempted

Crazy One More Time

I'm With You

Breathless

PINECONE VALLEY (Small Town Sexy Romance):

Love Me Again

Love Me Always

RETRIBUTION NOVELS (Sexy Romantic Suspense):

Branded

Hunted

Banished

Hijacked

Betrayed

ARGENT SPRINGS (Small Town Sexy Romance):

Whispers

Secrets

OTHER TITLES:

Moonlight and Margaritas

Sweet Vengeance

ABOUT THE AUTHOR

Award-winning author Cindy Stark lives in a small town shadowed by the Rocky Mountains. She enjoys creating magical mayhem in her witch cozy mysteries, unexpected twists in her emotional romantic suspense, and forever love with hot guys in her sexy contemporary romance stories.

She'd like to think she's the boss of her three adorable and sassy cats, but deep down, she knows she's ruled by kitty overlords. Someday, she hopes to earn enough to open a cat sanctuary where she can save all the kitties and play all day with toe beans and murder mittens.

Connect with her online at:
http://www.CindyStark.com
http://facebook.com/CindyStark19
https://www.goodreads.com/author/show/5895446.Cindy_Stark
https://www.amazon.com/Cindy-Stark/e/B008FT394W

Made in United States
Orlando, FL
22 March 2022

16052264R00104